Will's Hope

by Bonnie Ford Dunleavy

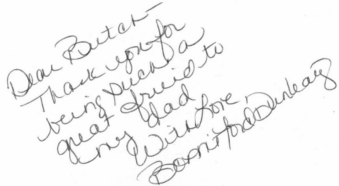

PublishAmerica
Baltimore

ISBN: 1-4241-1637-6
PUBLISHED BY PUBLISHAMERICA, LLLP
www.publishamerica.com
Baltimore

Printed in the United States of America

This book is dedicated to my dad, William Harry Ford; for without him, this story could not be told. Not only is *Will's Hope* based on actual events in my dad's life, but is inspired by his love for me, and his confidence in me. He has always been my rock and my beacon, without whom I might never have had the courage to write this book.

Dad, you were once a wild and crazy guy who had the good fortune to meet a wonderful young lady, our mom, Lorraine. God had a plan for you, and part of that plan included three baby girls, Becky, Bonnie and Betsy. Inundated by females, you remained the strong protector, but also the sensitive, caring father who (we always knew) would lay down his life for his girls. We always knew you'd be there for us, even through those all too often disappointing and difficult times. When we were little girls, we knew you were our shield, our shelter from the storms of life.

Thank you, Dad.

I love you with all my heart, and I am so blessed to have you as my father.

In Memory of

Larry Ford

My dad's youngest brother.

Uncle Larry,

Your dynamic wit, humor and sweet personality touched and blessed each of our lives immensely. You had an unbridled sense of life, so powerful and wondrous; it made life more fun for all of us.

Aunt Carol, you are much too young and vibrant to be widowed, and you will forever be in my prayers. Jill and Cindy, your dad's legacy will live on through you and your children. When we see each of you, we are able to see Larry, and you bless us.

We all miss you Uncle Larry
"You betcha!"

Acknowledgements

Just thanking each person who has been instrumental in the writing of this book seems so inadequate when I consider the time, dedication, encouragement and prayers each has contributed. I first have to thank my mom, Lorraine Ford. Without her, I would not have taken the leap of faith necessary for embarking on such an endeavor. Mom, not only did you encourage me, but you were also my first editor, and in so many ways, my writing partner. Thank you for the many hours you gave in order that *Will's Hope* could become a reality, and thank you that you never stopped believing in me, even when I doubted myself. Your kind and loving ways have been an unwavering and abiding inspiration to me. I love you.

Thank you, Dad, for being the captivating subject of this book. Obviously, without you there would not be a story to tell. May the readers of *Will's Hope* get at least a small glimpse of your wonderful qualities. Your strength of character and loving ways have endeared you to many. I love you immeasurably.

Very special thanks must go to my sister, Betsy, and her amazing husband, Gregg. It is also true that without them, this book would have only been a story residing in my imagination. Your editing expertise has added a wonderful flavor to *Will's Hope*. Thanks to Gregg, my intelligent brother-in-law who speaks computer with remarkable fluency, I was able to conquer some of my computer phobias. Betsy, the day you married Gregg, not only did the angels sing, but so did your sisters. To both of you, thank you, and I love you.

To my sister, Becky and her talented, husband, Tim, I must say thank you. Becky worked diligently to find a list of historical facts that helped define the character of Will. Tim, thank you for lighting up our lives with your smile and your kind and helpful ways. Your loving spirit speaks volumes to the world. I love you both and am blessed to have you in my life. Your prayers have been heard.

To my mother and father in law, Ed and Beverly Dunleavy, thank you for receiving me as your own. You always loved the little things I wrote, never seeing the flaws, but rather the message I was trying to convey. The communiqué of how greatly you love and the incredible family you've raised have been enormously instrumental in writing this book. Your encouragement has not gone unnoticed, and I love you for it. Thank you so much.

To all my girlfriends who have been like sisters to me: Patty, Leslie, Cappy, Nadia, Kathy, Debra, Barb, Mame, Mary, Jennifer, Jenny, Sue, Lisa, Maria, Diane, Suzette, Maritza and my closest friend and cousin, Lori, I extend my love and thanks. To Kimmi and her sweet husband, Paul, I thank you for being willing to work with an extremely camera-shy friend. Thank you, thank you, and thank you!

To the men in my life who have been like brothers, Hobie, Brad, Brian, Mike, Charlie and Chop, I love you guys! Thank you for being the brothers I was never fortunate enough to have while growing up.

A very special thank you must go to Publish America, for providing a home for my voice. I pray that many blessings will continue to be poured out to you, abounding and overflowing.

To my two beautiful, talented, and dynamic children, Kyle and Casey, I say thank you. Your blind faith in me makes me feel like I can do anything. Thank you for being my two biggest publicists, telling the world your mommy wrote a book. Your personalities make me proud; they shine brightly, revealing your abounding energy, compassion, and sincerity. Your happy confidence in tomorrow blesses me, and I love each of you more than I could ever express in words. But I'll say it anyway; I love you.

To my amazing, kind, loyal, patient and very handsome husband, Craig, thank you, thank you. Thanks for being so gracious and not complaining about the many evening hours I spent on the computer, rather than by your side, and for understanding when I said, "No, honey I can't go there today; I have to work on my book." Thank you for the smile that says you love me in spite of my ambitious dream. God must truly love me because he chose you for me. You're not only my husband, but you're my best friend. You are my emotional stabilizer, and the glue holding our family together. I love you with every fiber of my being. You bless me. I love you!

I may not be the best Christian example, but I know one thing for sure, there's a God who cares. So finally, I must thank my Heavenly Father, for without Him, nothing is possible. Only an amazing God could love me with all my faults. Thank You for all You have given me, and for the many ways You have blessed my life. Thank you that Your grace is sufficient. May my book, in some way, allow people to see how precious and essential You are. So, to my Lord and Savior I must say, thank you.

"For I know the plans I have for you," says the Lord. "They are plans for good and not for evil, to give you a future and a hope." Jeremiah 29:11

Contents

Prologue

It was the kind of morning that every cowboy anticipates while pondering the attributes of a horse race and its perfect scenario. Deep periwinkle-blue was the color of Kateyville's sky, with the sun glistening in bright shades of yellow and soft orange. It was Saturday, August 6, 1960, and Kateyville was experiencing an incredibly beautiful Adirondack morning. One could smell the natural compost of the pine trees, the dew drenched earth, and the familiar scent of the Raquette River with its fish and driftwoods. Every time the wind shifted, there was yet another wonderful combination of the same. The citizens of this northern New York town were gearing up for what was certain to be a spectacular quarter horse event.

A crowd of people had gathered together for what many were calling Kateyville's event of the year (and maybe even of a lifetime) for a young man named Will and his prized quarter horse, Sandy. As the race was about to begin, people were shuffling quickly into their seats straining for a glimpse of this much adored racing team. Will and Sandy had become hometown heroes of sorts and were favored to win.

An ardor of voices rose from the crowd, and binoculars were raised with nervous anticipation of things to come. Sandy seemed anxious as he tried to back away from the starting gate. The onlookers could faintly hear Will soothe him by saying, "Okay, Sandy! C'mon now boy; it's all right. This is our day. Stay calm, San. This one's for Dad." It was odd that Sandy would try to back out of the gate like that. Will had a difficult time convincing Sandy to get into place. One could only conclude that the size of the crowd and its accompanying noise shook

Sandy up a bit. Finally, Will was able to reassure and calm Sandy, allowing him to focus and prepare for the bell.

The bell sounded, and like steam from an old train whistle, the horses darted out of their gates. Sandy was the first one out. His hooves and those of the others pounded over the ground in unison, with a rapid paced clamor for the finish line. As each horse forged forward, dirt and muck scudded over the track in every direction.

Sandy was a magnificent sight, the smartest and most handsome quarter horse anyone would ever hope to see. He had long muscular legs, a wide chest, good lines, and large, bright eyes. His coat gleamed in the morning sun, revealing his rich chestnut color, while his lungs and noble heart began to work in unison to a steady rhythm. His muscular chest flexed with each tread around the track. Kateyville's loyal racing enthusiasts had their eyes fixed on Will and his prized, thoroughbred quarter horse.

William Casey turned eighteen years old just this past June, and he stood about 5 feet nine inches tall, weighing a very solid 165 pounds. He had short auburn hair, lively brown eyes, and a strong muscular build and seemed unaware, or at least unaffected, by his obvious good looks. Will came from a big family. He had one older brother, Jonathan, an older sister, Shannon, two younger brothers, Lenny and Christopher, and before she died, Will had a little sister named Sarah.

Very much his own person, Will usually didn't care a whole lot about people's opinion of him. Like most people, Will hoped others liked him; but, if they didn't, he just didn't worry about it. It was also true of Will that he didn't like to have anyone try to tell him who his friends should be. As long as people were genuine, Will liked them. He wasn't concerned about what station of life they came from. One could readily observe that he was an energetic, outgoing, fun-loving guy, all packaged in a kindly, but yet strong personality. He was a young man respected and liked by many.

This spirited young man never sat on the sidelines; he went after what he wanted and believed he could make things happen. Running races with his most valued friend, Sandy, just happened to be one of those endeavors he threw himself into. Will and Sandy loved to race, and they raced to win.

It was true that Will had a dynamic personality that drew people in; however, he also had a wild, untamed side that many times put him or others in danger. Even his own father had difficulty controlling Will in spite of their close relationship. That is, until he gave Will something very special.

Harry, Will's father, had always worried about where Will's wild streak would take him. The guilt and trauma of losing his little sister, Sarah, fueled Will's rebellion. Harry knew that, but he also feared something else might be at the root of his reckless behavior, something from Harry's past, and something he agonized over. This chapter of Harry's life was so traumatic and painful that he made an inner vow to keep it hidden and to never talk about it.

During his waywardness, Will took chances that seemed foolhardy and risky. It was a surprise, as well as a disappointment to many when Will exhibited this audacious and unbridled behavior. However, it was obvious to many that this brazen, dauntless spirit proved helpful when he and Sandy competed for a triumphant end to any horse racing competition. Never was he more determined and confident than today. The race was off to a good start, and Will and Sandy were in the lead.

Turning around, Will could see their amazing lead. Just as he started to measure the rest of the stretch in front of him, he felt a jerk from Sandy. Will's world collided with Sandy's as the spectators looked on in terror. A terrible accident began to be played out before the horror-stricken, helpless crowd. Sandy dropped to the ground as he abruptly rolled forward with Will never leaving the saddle. Falling to the ground, Sandy rolled and twisted in ways a horse was never meant to. William was trapped beneath him. This was not the first time Sandy's speed advanced him to the lead; but this time, being in front led to peril, not triumph. The other horses were unable to avoid the twisted wreckage and soon trampled Will and Sandy beneath their hooves. Before Will's face were crashing hooves and whipping tails! Desperate cries came from the other horsemen as they frantically tried to miss hitting Will and Sandy. "Whoa! Oh, boy! Jump girl! Oh, Lord, easy,

easy!" Their desperate cries were of no use. There was no way to control the horses or this deadly predicament.

Will's mouth was full of dirt, and just as he tried to spit it out, he felt a sharp thud come down on his head. Will's body became limp and motionless as it lay in an eerie stillness on the horse track.

From the stands, a still hush replaced the previous excitement. In the deafening silence, prayers reached forth to the heavens as fear and anguish masked hope. The onlookers, with hands cupped over their mouths and toes bent to the tips, strained desperate eyes trying to catch a glimpse of the fate of Will and Sandy. William lay lifeless and bloody on the ground beneath Sandy. Will's older brother, Jonathan, ran to the ill-fated scene. The fear on John's face told a horrifying story.

Panic permeated the air. Will was a young man that had overcome so much, even though uncertainty and adversity always seemed to loom over his life. Many in this small logging town had grown to admire and love Will. The idea that something terrible could happen to him now was unconscionable. It seemed such a short time ago that Will's family buried Sarah. She was born premature and sickly, and no one believed she would live. Sarah survived her infant years, only to lose her life at the untimely age of six. And it was only this past year that tragedy had delivered yet another terrible blow to Will and his family, and they had yet another loss to overcome. It was unthinkable that the Caseys would have to bear even more sorrow.

A crowd of people began to surround the accident where Will and Sandy lay. As Sandy desperately tried to stand, his head seemed to dangle uncontrollably to the side. Those who had even the slightest degree of equine knowledge knew Sandy had probably broken his neck, an injury that almost always leads to fatality. Sandy was writhing in pain. He was a 1200-pound quarter horse, Will's best friend, and he lay atop him.

Gregg Pace, the family's trusted friend, as well as Sandy's trainer, was the first to arrive on the scene. He gave Sandy something to help calm him down. Now, they both lay lifeless and the sight was agonizingly chilling.

Thankfully, an ambulance and several emergency personnel are always equipped and ready at a moment's notice during all horse racing and rodeo events, and this day was no exception. Within seconds, its siren sounded, and the ambulance was brought inside the track. Once inside the track, it seemed to take forever. Eventually, Will was lifted from the ground up into the ambulance and the crowd erupted in applause. Will was whisked away, with his fate yet unknown.

When the ambulance left the track, a special horse trailer was brought in to retrieve Sandy. Many men were needed to move him. Everyone watched as he was hoisted up into the trailer. Watching in horror, they could see Sandy's contorted, broken bones that once comprised his magnificent frame. Now, he was lifeless, bloody, and hauntingly still.

An expected triumph had turned to shock and disbelief.

Chapter 1
A Morning Ritual (Summer, 1959)

As soon as I entered the kitchen, I grabbed a large mug of milk, three of mom's doughnuts and a few sugar cubes for Sandy. I headed out to the barn. As I ambled across the yard, I could smell fresh cut hay, Mom's perennial garden and the clean, crisp scent of last night's rainfall. Lingering in the morning air was the intrusive aroma of cow dung that generously exploded on my olfactory senses.

The smell of cow manure drifted from most properties in Kateyville. Many of the boys around here were thankful for that, making it impossible to be singled out as the 'stinky kid' at school. "Cow droppings are like fine cologne around here, and all the popular boys in town wear it," my friend Bart Murray would jokingly say.

As I walked into the barn toward Sandy's stall, he began to nod his head up and down as if to say, "Hi, Will. I'm glad you're here!" His lips fluttered like the purr of a small engine and he was as happy to see me as I was him. Being accepted and loved by Sandy makes me feel special, even blessed. It's a trust I never want to break.

As I opened the door to Sandy's stall and patted him on top of the head, I greeted him like I would any good friend. "Hello, Sandy! How do you feel this morning? Did you get a good night's sleep? I sure did. I had a big bowl of ice cream last night before bed, and that always knocks me down for the count."

As I spoke, Sandy, listening intently, just peered at me through his brilliant brown eyes, tipping his head from side to side. I knew he completely understood the words I spoke, and he attentively read my every expression.

Sandy, Dad, and I watched the sun come up over the horizon nearly every morning. We took in the calm air, and the coolness rested in our noses like the scent of a fine bouquet of flowers. The only thing different about this morning was that Dad hadn't joined us.

"This is living, Sandy," I said. Once I drank my milk and finished off my last cinnamon-coated doughnut, I reached into my pocket to find the sugar cubes for Sandy. The routine of grabbing a mug of milk, a few doughnuts and sugar cubes for Sandy was barely ever missed.

As the sun began to steal over the field's horizon, Sandy and I stood quietly side by side, mesmerized by the beauty. As the sun inched up, its rays became brighter and brighter. During the early part of its accent, the sun glowed in colors of red and orange, but as it came into full view, it turned to blinding shades of white and yellow. Watching the sunrise, Sandy and I knew words spoken would only ruin the moment; and so, a young man and his horse quietly stood, sharing the spectacular view.

Over my shoulder, I was able to see Dad leave the house and get into his Buick. Dad gave me a great big wave and shouted that he would see me after school. "Make sure you give Sandy a good trot this morning, and be sure to not let the jitters get to you. You and Sandy will do just fine today. I love you!" And with a wave, he pulled out of the yard. Like I said, Dad usually drank his first cup of coffee with Sandy and me as we watched the sunrise, but apparently he was in too big of a rush this morning. Only something urgently important at work would keep him from our morning ritual. I was disappointed, but I also understood.

After our two-mile trot, I decided to give Sandy a good brushing to keep his fine chestnut coat shiny and bright. He enjoyed the rubdown and loved being brushed and pampered by me, and in return, he always gave me his absolute best on the track. Tryouts were after school, and I was sure Sandy knew it. He was well prepared and anxious to comply with the rigors of a race. It was thought by many in Kateyville that Sandy and I were a sure "shoe in," but Sandy and I preferred calling ourselves a sure "horseshoe in."

"Will, hurry up and get in here for breakfast! You need to get off to school in twenty minutes!"

I answered Mom, "I'm on my way." I ran into the house and headed straight for the bathroom. After washing my hands, I quickly directed my steps towards the table. Mom had made a breakfast of scrambled eggs, bacon and small, salt potatoes. This was my favorite breakfast combination, and mom knew it. She made it just for me, on this very important day.

Today was the qualifying race. If Sandy and I won this race, we would be off to the final competition that would lead us to the Grand Championship Quarter Horse Race of Kateyville County. Many thought we would win last year's race, but we lost by a nose. I'm sure it wasn't a secret to anyone that I foolishly ran the race with a fever of 103 degrees. Flu attacked my body the entire two weeks before the race, yet I still continued to run drills with Sandy. We practiced so much, even in the rain that I never allowed my body to recover in time for the race.

This year was our year; Sandy and I knew it. Nervousness came over me like a flood. I felt that I could use this energy to my advantage. "The jitters" that I was feeling was the kind of nervous anticipation that keeps you alert and on your toes. Sandy and I were ready to race, and many of our relatives and friends in Kateyville were ready to see us win.

Chapter 2
A Bit of History

I thought my school day would never end. All day I watched the clock. When 3 o'clock finally came, I was out the door quicker than you could say "quarter horse." With the race ahead, I couldn't get home fast enough. My usual route home always took me down Cayey Lane, Kateyville's main thoroughfare.

Along Cayey Lane, one can find many shops and businesses that give quaintness to our little town. Preserving history is notably important to the residents of Kateyville. Mandates, issued by the village's council members, order that each building must stay in keeping with guidelines that help safeguard the commemoration of the town's history and ancestry. Restoration and upkeep are "the order of the day" for our citizens. Most of the business owners concur with each proclamation and are more than happy to comply.

The history of Kateyville is renowned and goes as far back as the early 1800's. In the local Kateyville Museum, many famous people are celebrated due to the impact they had on our town's history. Among those who've been honored is Dr. Harvey Thatcher. While living in nearby Potsdam in 1884, he invented one of the early milk bottles with its ingenious wire closure. That may seem like a small thing to some, but we here in Kateyville are very proud of the man.

One of the goals of the museum is to celebrate the folk art and its talented artists, by displaying their decoys, books, woodcarvings, and antique Amish quilts. The exhibit has also preserved some sweet grass baskets made by some of the Mohawk Indians that once resided here.

The many preserved artifacts proudly reveal the talent, ingenuity and dedicated workmanship of our former citizens.

One of my dad's favorite artists of the past was named Fredric Remington. He was a famous artist, born in 1861. Mr. Remington was well renowned for his magnificent sculptures that depicted the life of hard working people of that time. Dad often reminded me that we wouldn't have what we appreciate today if it weren't for those hard working folks. Before Fredric Remington moved west, he lived in nearby Ogdensburg, NY, where there is a museum dedicated to him. Our museum displays a few bronze sculptures he created. Some of his earlier works illustrated life in the North Country, while his later works revealed the people and life of the Old West.

This part of the country was once known as "The Gateway to the North" and had been a very busy place, bustling with new settlers every week. This gateway was marked with the historic Sunday Rock, located in our southern end. It is rumored that law and order existed north of Sunday Rock, but lawlessness was tolerated south of it. Many businesses provided sustenance for the people of this area as far back as the mid to late 1800's, such as foundry and machine shops, flouring mills, furniture shops and tanneries. In fact, around 1850, the largest tannery in the state could be found here, producing 40,000 hides of leather per year. But before tanneries were big around here, lumbering and dairying ruled the land. Because our father owned a lumber mill, we were curious as to who was responsible for building the first one in our area. While doing a bit of research, we found that Edward Crary built the first sawmill in the vicinity in 1837. And thanks to the opening of the Northern Railroad, the lumber industry skyrocketed.

The majestic Raquette River runs through our town. Ten miles north of us, the Raquette River Paper Company was built in February, 1891. The power to run the mill was generated from five large water wheels. Our ancestors were hard working people who endured long, cold winters but enjoyed ideal climate in our spring, summer, and fall months.

While researching our area, it was very interesting to note that many of the names pulled from the 1820's are names we still hear in the area today, such as, A. Barton Hepburn, Hawley, Jesse Colton Higley, and Hiram Pierce. A. Barton Hepburn was born in Kateyville and later moved to New York City. There he made his fortune on Wall Street. He was proud of his roots and never forgot the people of the North Country. A beautiful, granite-stone, Hepburn Library can be seen in the center of our town. He funded the building of six other libraries that can be found in neighboring towns. A nursing school in Ogdensburg, NY was also named after him. The Clarkson family of Potsdam donated funds to have the impressive, sandstone, Episcopal Church built across from the library. This church was built in loving memory of Elizabeth Clarkson, a strong supporter of the Episcopal Church in Kateyville. This wealthy family also funded the development of Clarkson University, located in Potsdam. It should be dually noted that Clarkson University has become one of the most prestigious colleges in the country, especially for its engineering department.

Many of our streets and towns have been named after an earlier pioneer, Jesse Colton Higley, as well as a man by the name of Hiram Pierce who founded the nearby town of Piercefield.

One of my favorites from earlier times was a pirate by the name of Bill Johnston. Pirate Bill acted as an American spy during the War of 1812 while sailing on the nearby St. Lawrence River. His fearless, cunning ways provided vital information to the Americans and has made Kateyville citizens proud to call him "a friend from the past."

Not only is the museum a place of guarded historical memories, it is also representative of the architecture found throughout the village. Many sidewalks are still laden with cobblestone, and the buildings are early sandstone, brick or an exact replica of slat-wood siding. The slat-wood buildings are decorated with flower baskets, shutters and fancy, hand-carved molding that was once a proud representation of the type of craftsmanship found in the early 1800's. The village of Kateyville and its residents take historical preservation very seriously.

Along my run home, I passed the Kateyville Post Office, Griffin's Veterinary Hospital, Leslie's Beauty Shop and The Hide-Away Diner. On the opposite side of the street, one can see Dave's Jewelry Store, Pitco's Pharmacy, and Cowper's Café. And one of the town's most heavily trafficked places is Braun's German Bakery, where its specialty, elephant ear cookies, is baked fresh everyday. They must be ordered in the morning because the supply is often exhausted before lunch.

Hoffman's House for Troubled Youth stands on the corner of Cayey Lane and Bennett Road. The original owner of Hoffman's House, Leo Hoffman, built the structure to house soldiers during the War of 1812. Many of the soldiers had been aboard ships, fighting along Lake Champlain, and while traveling from the North down to New York City, they used Hoffman's place as a stop-off point to rest.

On the opposite end of town, resides Kateyville Hospital, famous for its critical care unit, trauma center and "state of the art" research laboratory. Some of the finest and smartest doctors to come out of medical school work at our hospital.

As I ran past each business, doors swung open and friends and fans began to shout flattering words of encouragement. By the looks of things, you would have thought the President of the United States and his motorcade were passing through our village. Humbled and honored was how they made me feel. I could hardly believe how gracious the people of this town were as they cheered Sandy and me on in this way.

"This is your year, Will! Blow their hats off!" shouted Ken from the post office.

"Give Sandy a kiss for me, Will, a kiss for good luck!" yelled Janet Braun.

"After you win that race Will, get your handsome self in here for a haircut; unless of course, that fast paced Sandy blows your hair clean off your head!" shouted Leslie. That was Leslie for you; she had a way with words, and she always knew how to make me laugh. As I gave her a wave, a big smile curled across my face.

"Dinner's on me tonight, Will. Give 'em all you've got!" yelled out Ed from The Hide-Away.

Even the boys at Hoffman's House shouted out their hopes for a win.

"Go get 'em, Will!"

"Show 'em what it really means to ride!"

"Let Sandy loose to show off his stuff!"

As I glanced past the Hoffman House, I realized it had been only by God's grace that I never landed there myself. Lord knows, I would have earned it.

My heart was racing with anxious expectation, but as I heard the voices of friends and neighbors, my jitters turned to excitement. This was our big day, a day for Sandy and me. I just knew we were ready. Never before had I felt more confident. Sandy was well prepared to run, and I was primed to ride. Dad once told me that he thought Sandy's and my heart beat as one when I rode him. I think he's right. We loved to race with the wind, while listening to the sound of pounding hoofs and a cheering crowd, each of us with thoughts of victory playing in our mind. So often Dad would say, "You need horse sense and riding skill, but just as importantly, you must have a heart for racing. Without heart, you may win; but without the passion, sooner or later, your losses would start to outnumber the wins." I never believed for one minute that my passion for racing would end. I couldn't imagine anything that was able take that away, but I also knew I couldn't look into the future to see what lay ahead.

Once I arrived home, Mom had all of my gear out and ready. Even at seventeen, she still tended to baby me. She told me on more than one occasion, "You'll always be my baby, no matter how old you get." I have to say that I love and respect my mom, and I would never take advantage of her occasional codling. Especially because there was a time when it seemed that all I ever did was take advantage of her, as well as the other people who loved and cared for me.

After a terrible accident happened to my little sister, Sarah, something inside me changed, a change not for the better. When she died, I blamed myself. I believed for sure it was my fault, and there wasn't a soul who could tell me any differently. The grief I felt after losing her clouded my vision. I had a hard time seeing any value in my life. For a long time after Sarah's death, my living became wild and reckless because honestly, I just didn't care. It took something very special to get me to appreciate all that I had been given. That something special was given to me by my Mom and Dad; they gave me Sandy, my faithful friend and horse. Sandy stole my heart and changed my life.

After running into the house and changing into my riding clothes, I threw my chaps over my shoulder. I grabbed my lucky handkerchief and the cowboy hat that had only been worn by one other person than me, my dad. I proudly placed it on my head and headed back downstairs. My dad had given me that cowboy hat before last year's race. Even though I hadn't won that race, I still walked with pride and joy. I understood the significance of that hat, and knew there was no other way that I could walk while wearing his dashing brim.

Wearing Dad's hat meant more to me than anyone would ever know. When he gave it to me, I knew it was more than just a kind gesture. I saw for the first time that Dad was proud of me, and he loved me no matter what I had done, or in Sarah's case, hadn't done. After all the crazy, dangerous and stupid things I did during my stint of rebellion, to have my father proud of me was a gift so large its value could never be measured. I was the prodigal son who had returned home, and he clearly represented the father welcoming me back. We became proof that a newfound relationship of love and respect can be rekindled between a father and a son.

Whenever Sandy and I went out for a ride or a practice run, I wore that hat, and I wore it with gratitude. Attached to my cherished hat was a broach, a broach that once belonged to Sarah. It's really just the simplest little thing—a small red rose made of glass, but it wasn't simple to Sarah. She loved it. It pains me every time I look at it, but I have to wear it. It makes me feel closer to her somehow.

After a long, difficult struggle, I truly believe that I have finally started to mature and think of others as Dad hoped I would. Along with his confidence in me, I could sense his unconditional love. It humbles me to understand how much he really does care. Dad knew the root of my bad ways, and he would always find those perfect moments to try and reassure me that I had done all I could do to save Sarah. Somehow, my relationship with Sandy enabled me to let go of my guilt and self-hatred. I was beginning to feel some peace and hope for good days ahead.

Before my rebellious period, my dad and I had always been close, but now we were closer than ever. Spending time together with Sandy made us even closer. Everything I knew about Sandy and racing, I learned from him. We spent hours, running drills, riding the woods and fields and just plain talking about stuff. Confiding in Dad had become easy and natural for me. For a lot of my friends, it was hard for them to talk with their parents; I knew I was lucky to not have to feel that way.

Harry Casey had been a championship, quarter-horse rider back when he was seventeen, and I would like to believe he passed that skill on to me. The love of horses gave us a connection that each of us treasured. The happiest times of my youth have been spent with Dad by my side. We continue to share a love of horses and a love of racing, and now we're able to experience a relationship grounded in mutual respect and admiration for one another. Deep in my heart, there's been a desire to be just like my dad, a man of courage, fortitude and compassion. I'm going to do my best to be like him, and I never want to disappoint him again.

Through his example, Dad has been able to teach my brothers, my sister Shannon, and me many things. He has always demonstrated devotion and loyalty toward our mom, frequently referring to her as the love of his life. And throughout the years, Dad was never too shy to tell each of us how much he cared for us. He has always known how to live in the moment and to enjoy others, feeling life should be fun for not just him, but also for the people he loved and cared about. Even though he desired life to be fun, he also knew when to be serious. He knew when it was time to extend the hand of grace and understanding and when he needed to be firm and stand his ground.

"Love believes all things" is an adage that came from his lips on many an occasion. I remember the day I asked him what exactly that meant. This was a couple of years ago. We were outside sitting on the front porch. I had been upset with my friend, Bart, because he went on a bike ride with one of his other friends, and he hadn't asked me to go. In school, Bart told me he would call me before they headed out, so we could meet up on the bike trail between his house and mine. He never called.

Dad took that as a perfect opportunity to explain what, "love believes all things" meant. He told me that we shouldn't be too quick to jump to conclusions about people, especially the important people in our life. We may think we have the answer to why a person acts in a certain way, or why they say what they say, but love asks us to believe the best in people—believe their motives are pure.

Later that evening, I found out that Bart did call, but Lenny told him I wasn't home. Dad was right; I should have believed the best when it came to Bart. Bart had been a true friend, and true friends don't intentionally hurt you. That small piece of advice has proven to help me on more than a few such occasions since then.

I'm so glad I finally wised up, and decided to listen to what my Dad had to say. It takes a lot of courage to admit your dad knows more about life than you do. Giving up my pride and rebellion has afforded me knowledge that will help me my entire life, and I truly hope that, in some way, I am on my way to becoming more like my dad.

Chapter 3
The Race, the Tragedy

Sandy, what an amazing American, quarter horse! He has always been known for his superb speed and excellent athletic ability. Rarely did Sandy ever lose a race, but once in a while, something unexpected would happen, causing him to lose his enthusiasm. For example, too much rain causes a lot of thick mud, and heavy mud is one of those things that can make racing difficult for Sandy. Some horses love that mud, but not Sandy. He has never been a "mudder".

Unfortunately, one of Sandy's loses included last year's qualifying, but he wasn't to blame; I was. The most disappointing aspect of that loss was that it cost us the chance to run in the Kateyville Grand Championship Quarter-Horse Race that was held in August of last year.

I truly believe that if we had gotten the chance to run the race (with me in better physical health), Sandy and I would have won the qualifying. Not only did I believe that, so did my friends, family and most of Kateyville. Disbelief and bewilderment was felt all over Kateyville when Sandy and I didn't win.

Sandy always shot out of his gate like lightening. He hadn't met a horse who could beat his starting time. Once out of his gate, all I ever had to do was lead Sandy in the proper direction, and with keen racing intuition and raw determination, Sandy would race to win.

The time had come for us to try to qualify again, and instead of racing with daunting weakness, we raced with confidence, strength and skill. Just before the race, an incredible fluttering kind of knowing rose up in my chest as I believed this year's qualifying belonged to Sandy and me. It was our day! This feeling was in stark contrast to last year's mood. All I felt then was unnerving uncertainty along with the body aches that often come with a case of the flu.

The track was a flurry of people as every seat in the bleachers seemed to be taken. You could easily see that the spectators were aflame with eagerness. Upon arrival, I looked up into the stands with a new realization of what was at stake. All along, I felt there was no way we could lose, but for mere seconds, I had allowed myself thoughts of "what if." I was ready for one of Dad's pep talks; I searched the crowd hoping to spot him. Dad had never been late for a race, and the fact that he hadn't shown up yet, worried me. I remember trying to brush my uncomfortable feelings aside and stay focused on the race. It was important to temper all negative emotion that could weaken my concentration and possibly destroy our chances for a win. I also didn't want Sandy to sense my anxiety. This day was not only my day, but it belonged to Sandy as well.

Gregg Pace had been a family friend for a very long time, and it was he that led Sandy and me toward the starting gate. As we began our approach, Sandy and I did a quick side trot; I lifted my hat and gave a small wave to the crowd. This was our customary signature.

Deliberate silence permeated the stadium. The still hush was an understood display of respect and a kind of racing etiquette.

Ready for the starting bell, each horse was lined up and ready. It was a magnificent sight to see. Sandy was the only chestnut horse in the line. Jake Eisenhower was the color of buckskin, In the Saddle was red dun, Stand Alone was grullo, Have Faith was palomino, Evening Rose was red roan and the rest were the color of sorrel. Each horse stood strong, steady and ready for the ride.

Before the bell sounded, I took one more look around trying to find my dad. I could see my mom, each of my brothers, and my sister, Shannon. It was strange to see them all standing there without Dad; he never missed a race. Just before the bell sounded, I experienced a strange feeling, as if something were terribly wrong. Yet, as quickly as the emotion came, it was fast to leave.

The bell sounded, and Sandy was the first one out. He instantly left the outside track and moved to the inside lane tapering the center circle. This was the best position for a horse to be in to win a race. It was now up to Sandy to give it all he had. As he ran, his legs resembled the wheels of a speeding locomotive. Sandy had the power, strength and unbeatable will to win. Have Faith and Sandy ran neck-and-neck. Each horse was trying desperately to nudge into the lead. Seeing the finish line ahead, I looked down at Sandy, and I knew what was coming. Sandy peered out of the corner of his eye at Have Faith, as if to say, "See ya!" With a thrust of muscular vigor, Sandy bolted into the lead, leaving Have Faith at least two horse lengths behind!

Sandy was the first to cross the finish line! The crowd erupted with applause and shouts of exuberant joy. We had won the race with Have Faith coming in second, In the Saddle third, and Jake Eisenhower fourth. Sandy and I had finally done it! Victory felt so incredibly sweet, and we were now finally on our way to the Kateyville Grand Championship Quarter-Horse Race.

During our victory lap, Sandy was given a wreath of red carnations he proudly wore around his neck. As our lap was coming to an end, Gregg Pace came out to lead us off the track. As I was leaving, I continued to look for Dad. I wasn't able to see him anywhere.

If Dad wasn't in the stable area, something was definitely wrong. He always reached Sandy's stable before we got there.

I was getting an anxious feeling, and I felt like there were knots in my stomach. This feeling was so overpowering that I no longer cared about the win. "Gregg, have you seen Dad anywhere?"

"No, Will, I haven't. I'm sure he's out there somewhere. You know he would never miss one of your races." Gregg sounded encouraging.

"Yeah, I know, Gregg, and that's what's got me worried."

I headed out to find my mom. As soon as I spotted her, I quickly headed her way. On my way, I saw Officer Dan Hopkins also walking toward my mom. When Officer Hopkins saw me coming, he stood silently next to Mom, waiting for me to join them.

I took off my hat and reached out my hand to greet Officer Hopkins. "Hello Officer. How are you?"

Officer Hopkins spoke with obvious distress in his voice. "Well, Will, I need to speak to you and your family about something." Turning his eyes towards Mom, he continued, "It's about Harry."

"What do you mean? What's happened to Dad? Dan? I don't like this." I rambled, panicked at what he had to tell us.

Jonathan spoke up, "Will, calm down. Let Dan explain."

As Officer Hopkins began to speak, I couldn't believe what I was hearing. "I'm so sorry Mrs. Casey, but something has happened to Harry. Harry and I have always been close, and I wanted to be the one to tell you."

"Tell me what, Dan?" Mom's words were shaky and hardly audible.

As the details of my dad's accident began to be told, Mom started to tremble uncontrollably. It wasn't long before she collapsed into Jonathan's arms and began to sob.

I was numb; I couldn't feel a thing. No tears came; I just felt shock and disbelief. Thoughts began to swirl around inside my head; there's no way Dad could be gone. This couldn't be happening. Please, Lord; please tell me this is all a huge mistake.

Before Officer Hopkins left, he had tears in his eyes and choked out words as best he could. He said that he didn't believe Dad had suffered. It happened so quickly that he was sure Dad hadn't felt a thing. Officer Hopkins explained how it happened. Dad had parked his car along the side of the street. As Dad stepped out of his car, a cement truck was passing by. As soon as he turned around, it was all over. There had been a pipe sticking out beyond the frame of the truck. The pipe caught the lapel on Dad's coat and forced him under the vehicle. His body landed right in front of the back wheels, and in an instant, our dad was gone.

Mom desperately tried to compose herself. She selflessly knew this had been an important day for Sandy and me. Mom sadly understood that my exhilarating moment of victory had turned into horror and sadness. She told me that Dad would have been real proud of Sandy and me. That was all she had the strength to say. I told her the race wasn't important; all that mattered was our family.

I couldn't move; I just stood there. Jonathan helped Mom to the car. Thankfully, Lenny and Christopher weren't there. Susan, Jonathan's wife, had taken them to buy a hot dog right after the race; so, they never heard what Officer Hopkins had come to say.

Dad's hat was in my hand. I looked at it for a moment and then squeezed it close to my chest. As I did, I could smell that familiar scent of sawdust, motor oil, and traces of the cologne Dad liked to wear. I felt as if my feet were cemented to the ground. After trying desperately to move, I was finally able to head for Sandy's stall. Once I got there, I hugged him hard around the neck. It was then that I could no longer hold back the tears. All I could do was cry. I told Sandy that Dad was gone. My words, stammering through tears, had soon become a whisper. "How's my life going to be now, Sandy? What will I do? I'm lost without Dad."

As I spoke to Sandy, my heart pounded in a way I thought would make me pass out. I was in a panic like I never felt before, and my words began to shake with each syllable. "Oh, Sandy, I don't want this to be true. I want Dad back. I want him back. He wasn't just my dad; he was my friend."

I was glad Sandy was there, I knew that I needed him more than ever. If a horse could convey a message, Sandy gave one of caring and understanding as he brushed his head against mine.

The race was held on a Friday, and by Tuesday Dad had been laid to rest. Before the start of the funeral, people arrived in droves. Seven years ago, I was only ten, but I remember many things about that year. I vividly remembered the day of Sarah's funeral. As I looked at all the cars coming to pay tribute, it reminded me of all those who had come to say goodbye to Sarah.

It was hard for me to believe so many people could have known our dad. In his lifetime, he touched so many peoples' lives. Each person I spoke to seemed to be saying the same things.

"Your Dad was a good man, an honest man, a man of his word."

"He'd give you the shirt off his back."

"Your dad always looked for the good in people."

"I never heard him speak an unkind word about anybody."

"Your dad worked harder than any man I've known."

We also had a few people who felt they needed to include Sarah in all of this.

"Now, your Dad can be with Sarah."

"I'm sure Sarah is in your dad's arms right now."

"Now, you have two people looking down on you, Will, your dad and Sarah."

The grief of losing Dad was hard enough, but people thinking they had to bring Sarah into the middle of it, just doubled the size of my heartache. I'm sure they meant well, but I just didn't see it that way. Guilt was at the root of those feelings; I was sure of it, and I just couldn't go there right then. I hated the guilt.

Dad had 300 men working for him, and they all came to pay their respects. As these men passed by Dad's casket, there wasn't a dry eye among them. It was plain to see that they would truly miss him. Dad said they were like family to him, and that he would do anything he could to help any one of them if they needed it.

I started to remember back to the time Barney Stalters' house burned down. Dad took Barney and his family in until they were able to finish building their new house. There was another time when a friend was in need. George Plummer came into some financial trouble. Before he worked for our dad, George's wife had gotten real sick. They didn't have health insurance, and so the bills became more than the Plummer's could handle. Dad hired George and gave him a good salary, along with health insurance. Shortly thereafter, Dad secretly paid the hospital all that the Plummer family owed. Everyone knew it was my dad, but he would never admit to it.

Eventually, the funeral service given for my dad at his graveside came to an end. As the last of the cars left the graveyard, Jonathan took Mom and the other kids home. I took this time to be alone with my dad. It was now my turn to say goodbye. As I stood there next to Dad's grave, my eyes slowly shifted to the adjacent marker which read "Sarah Shane Casey, 1946-1952, daughter of Harry and Claire Casey". I thought I had made my peace with Sarah and her death, but I found myself overwhelmed with grief.

After Sarah died there were so many emotions I had to get past.

Definitely guilt was my biggest obstacle, but so was control. Part of me refused to give up my grief, because in doing so, I believed I might forget about Sarah. The memory of what she looked like, acted like and sounded like might disappear forever. Strangely, the pain I felt for her loss kept me connected to her. Throughout my grief, Sarah's features resonated within my soul.

Sarah dying left me with many questions. The biggest question I had at the time was, "How could I just go on trying to live a normal life?" In my mind, that wouldn't be fair to Sarah. Her life was over; she couldn't go on as "normal." I also hated to see other people just going on with their lives. Didn't they know Sarah was dead and that we were suffering? If we allowed life to go on as usual, she would become only a memory. When I began to heal, I realized that the only thing linking us to Sarah was just that, our memory of her, and that was something I was never going to lose.

Oh, yes, surprisingly, I still believed in God, but I wasn't sure he cared for me much. I believed in His existence, none the less. Eventually, I consoled myself by believing that I would see Sarah again, in Heaven. I knew with all my heart, if Heaven truly did exist, Sarah would be there.

Losing my father was a different kind of grief. The gnawing ache in my heart told me that I had another long, difficult haul ahead of me. As I looked down at Dad's casket, I poured my heart out to him, "Dad, I don't know how I am going to be able to get through this. You and I had finally become real friends. I could go to you whenever I had a problem or just had something I needed to figure out. You were always there to listen and give me direction. The advice you gave seemed to come so naturally to you. No matter what the situation was, or what I needed help with, you had an answer. Your answer usually brought light to the dark tunnel of my circumstances. Your advice eventually helped me make sense of things. I say eventually, because I didn't always accept your advice right away. With a great deal of trial and error, I finally learned that I would have a lot less distress in my life if I acquiesced sooner to your advice, rather than later.

"When Sarah died, you knew how guilty I felt. You could have blamed me, but you didn't. You reached out to me with your incredible compassion and assured me that it wasn't my fault. Deep inside, I selfishly worried you would hate me because I lived, and Sarah didn't. Do you remember the question I asked you? I asked how you could possibly love me now? You assured me that your love for me was for always, and nothing would ever change that. You said your heart was broken, and that you would always miss and long for Sarah, but that would never lessen your affection for me. I didn't believe you. I thought you said all that just to console me. It took me a long time before I realized you meant every word you said and that you truly did love me.

"When Sarah died, you never placed blame; your love for me didn't change or lessen. It almost seemed that you cared for me more. The grief and guilt I felt for Sarah caused me to go in a direction you feared I might go in, but you never gave up on me. Without your love and support, my stone could very well be here as well. Thank you, Dad, for everything. And Dad, thank you for Sandy. We will visit as often as we can."

I ran back to the car, grabbed something from the backseat, and ran back to Dad's graveside. "Here, Dad. This is from Sandy." On his tombstone, I placed the ring of carnations Sandy received after the race. Sandy's carnations had barely wilted, and amazingly looked as fresh as the day of the race, making them appear to not only be for Sandy, but for Dad as well.

"I want you to know that I will take good care of Mom. She's really going to need me now. Mom has told us many times that her family was her life. I remember some of the things she often said about you, things like: 'Oh, I'm blessed. I married the love of my life.' Or, 'It doesn't matter how long we've been together, my heart still goes pitter-patter when he enters the room.' I knew you felt the same way about her. I think it was in the way you looked at her. I sometimes caught you staring at her as she puttered around the kitchen. You adored her; I could tell. Not many men would leave love notes around for their wife to find, but you did. I admired you for that. Being romantic was something you didn't shy away from. You made Mom happy."

I stood there for a while remembering back to the life Mom and Dad shared. Realizing things will never be the same again for any of us, but especially for Mom. I began to talk to Dad again, "How's Mom going to make it without you? I promise you; I will do all that I can to help. When Sarah died, Mom was devastated. I really thought she would die from grief, but you comforted her, loved her, and never tried to hurry her heartache away, even though seeing her pain, made yours all that much more difficult to bear. I remember something you said. You and I were sitting outside, and both of us could hear Mom crying through her bedroom window. You said you wished you could protect her and make all of her pain go away, but only time and grace would do that. I knew you were hurting as much as she was, but you never let that show. The love you two shared seemed to grow during that time. You explained that difficult times can drive people apart or draw them closer. I still marvel at how you two were able to stay strong enough to continue loving the people in your life that still needed you."

"Jonathan said you were Mom's rock, her covering in a time of great despair, and he was right. So, I vow to you today that I will do my best to be that for her now, her rock and covering. Also, be contented in knowing that I will help her look after the kids, especially Christopher and Lenny."

"Rebellion was the faulty antidote I used for dealing with Sarah's death, but you can be sure that's not the case this time. I will come through this a better man, and I have you to thank for that, Dad. If I were to do anything less, it would be showing you disrespect, and I won't do that."

I decided to sit down. Sitting on the ground, I picked at the grass as I thought about Dad. "I've been doing some thinking, Dad. I think I've decided that I'm not going to race anymore. You and I shared racing, the rodeo and horses. Sandy doesn't just belong to me; he belongs to you, too. I can't imagine doing any of it without you."

I sat there quiet for a very long time, and then I spoke again. All I could say was, "Why'd you go, Dad? Why? I'm really going to miss you. I'll always love you." I slowly got up while looking at the hat Dad gave me. With tears in my eyes, I put it on and walked away.

Chapter 4
Jonathan Takes Over

It had been less than a month since Dad passed away. Jonathan stepped in and took over the Lumber Company. He had been working with Dad for over two years now and knew every rope of the business. Dad had intended to retire sometime in the near future, and he wanted to be sure the business would be well taken care of. He chose the right man when he chose Jonathan.

When it came to personality traits, Jonathan and Dad really weren't much alike. This was apparent in the way people described each of them. I began to remember back to some of the things people had said about Dad, "Oh, Harry, he was one of the most charismatic fellas I've ever met. He was an outgoing, fun loving guy, and boy, what a quipster. He could tell jokes better than anyone I know. His descriptive monologues would have you sitting on the edge of your seat with incredible anticipation, and then he'd slam you with the punch line. Everyone within earshot would be roaring with laughter."

"Now, Harry is a super guy, but boy oh boy, if you cross him or harm someone close to him, you had better watch out. There was a side to Harry that only the most daring would be willing to reckon with. Understand, however, Harry was always fair; only those deserving were subject to his volatile, 'take care of business' side."

"One of the greatest qualities that Harry had was undying loyalty. He was a sincere, genuine friend—the best any person could ever hope to have."

"Harry was a man of remarkable faith. He attended St. Mary's

Church nearly every Sunday. He was never ashamed to say he kept a Bible on his nightstand, and in private moments spent with his God, he often prayed."

"Sentimental, romantic, passionate and fervent were words that could describe Harry. Planning romantic dates and trips with Claire had always been one of his favorite things to do. He loved her with all his heart."

I'll never forget the conversation I heard in the mill one day. I had been reading a book in the back corner of the mill waiting for Dad to finish work. Only Dad knew I was there. I had finished one of my chapters and decided to take a break from my reading. As I was looking around the room, I saw Mr. Braves. He was talking to one of the other guys. Still to this day I remember the sound of his voice as he spoke about Dad, "Boy, that Harry loves his kids; he'd do anything for them. One of the most heartbreaking moments I remember Harry experiencing was when he lost his little girl, Sarah. He was a broken man. That scene will be forever etched in my memory. The funeral had just ended, and people were starting to leave. Sarah's casket had been suspended above the ground where her grave had been dug. As they began to lower the casket into the ground, Harry dropped to his knees, touched the casket with his hand, bent his head down to the ground, and he began to sob. He knew that once that casket was lowered in the ground, a heavy finality would set in. He couldn't bear that final goodbye."

I was young then, but I remember Dad doing that. Seeing him so brokenhearted made me hate myself all the more. I felt like I had done that to him.

I once overheard a man talking about my dad in the town's diner. He said, "Harry's family means more to him than anything else. I dare say that he probably works as hard as he does, just for them.

I am at a loss for words to describe exactly how great I think my dad was.

Now, getting back to how different my dad and Jonathan are, this is what someone might say about Jonathan, "He's rather reserved, a quiet kinda guy."

Some would say, "He's introspective, a thinker and an analyzer."

"Jonathan has strong likes and equally strong dislikes."

Susan, Jonathan's wife has said, on more than one occasion, "Oh, Jonathan, he's not the best communicator, always keeping his feelings hidden from view. 'I love you' isn't said very often, but somehow, even with the lack of words, he's able to convey how deeply he loves me."

Mom says that he's cautious, not a big risk taker, but confidently resolute when a decision has been made. She felt that when it comes to business, he's all business, uncompromising and determined.

It is obvious to her that he is definitely not the disorderly type. On more than one occasion, I have heard Mom say, "Jonathan is a well kept, handsome young man who always dresses sharply, right down to his socks and shoes. He irons his own blue jeans and undershirts. One could say that he pays close attention to detail; nothing gets by him."

I think the most important and binding character traits shared by both my dad and Jonathan are honesty, loyalty, fairness and a strong work ethic. They each possessed a single eye bent on the completion of whatever task was at hand. If there was a job to be done, they were both determined to get it done, and done well. They both possessed wills of iron, and a long stubborn streak, but this never prevented them from trying to do the right thing. Each of them has always been willing to lend a hand where needed, and give respect where respect was earned.

Every now and then, I stopped by the mill to see Jonathan. Many times I found him sitting at Dad's old desk, just staring out the window. I sensed that this transition had been much harder on him than any of us realized. Sadness and grief gave even more definition to his wrinkled brow. This serious and thoughtful expression of his would last until he saw someone coming; he never wanted anyone to see his pain. Suddenly catching a view of someone, would cause him to straighten his stance. Many times he would blow and then wipe his nose, acting as if pepper or pollen were aggravating his senses. Never would he allow anyone, especially me, to view his pain. If he saw me looking, his response was usually the same, "Hey Will, how are ya doing? Man, the sawdust around here is really irritating me today."

I never revealed that I knew he was suffering. I just answered him saying I was fine, all the while hiding my true feelings as well.

The atmosphere at the mill had really changed. It used to be that when I came by to see Dad, the guys were almost always in a good mood. I would be greeted with lively hellos by everyone. Light conversation would be exchanged, along with a few jokes. A lot of laughter often ensued. I remember that before many jokes were told, 'the coast would have to be cleared.' If mom, or any other woman, were present, the quip couldn't be told. My dad always said, "Only a gentleman can truly banter. A joke isn't funny if it offends a lady."

Now, whenever I stopped by Dad's mill, the guys were kinda quiet and somber. They were still friendly, saying hello and stuff, but they sure weren't the same. It isn't hard to tell that the men really miss my dad. From the looks of things, I think it's going to take a long while for any of them to begin acting anything like they used to.

For me, the brief amount of time that's passed hasn't lessened my anguish any. Dad's death was so sudden that none of us seemed to be able to find a way to adjust. I can't tell you how many times, while standing outside with Sandy watching the sunrise, that I instinctively looked toward the back door expecting Dad to come out and join us. When Dad was here, rarely did either of us miss out on this daily morning routine. Dad almost always enjoyed his first cup of coffee with Sandy and me. I often took pleasure in my milk and doughnuts, while Sandy wallowed in contentment just to have us there with him.

Once the sun was finally up, Dad and I would exchange some light conversation. He sometimes imparted some pearls of wisdom. His advice usually had something to do with living today and not worrying about tomorrow. He offered pep talks about how the Lord intended us to live our very best today and give the worries of tomorrow to Him. I wondered what words of insight he would've had for me. Right then, I was just trying to get through the day. When the day is so dreary, it's hard to have optimistic thoughts about tomorrow. Yet, you can bet that if I knew how to give my dread of tomorrow to the Lord, I certainly would have.

John still hadn't seen me coming. He was off to that place in his mind that I understood all too well. The combined emotions of shock, sadness and loneliness, mixed in with the obvious worry about those around us, have given all of us a lot to think about. Uneasiness and gloom had settled over the mill like a heavy, dark mist.

"Hi, John. How's it going?" I asked.

"Oh hey, Will," as Jonathan wiped his nose, "I didn't see you walk in. How was school today?"

"Just more of the same," I unenthusiastically answered.

I have never liked school much. Sitting at a desk all day has always been rather torturous for me. I'm just not the kind of guy who finds it easy to learn while sitting still. I like to be up and around, getting my hands dirty. Science is my highest grade, a B+. I like working in the science labs where I can actively solve problems by performing experiments, getting my hands into it. I also like to read, but only if I can choose the subject. Mom thinks my grades should be better, and she might be correct. I'm afraid my grades are rather substandard, a standard I am perfectly happy with.

Mom said my teachers were generally amazed at my vocabulary, given my average grades. She told them that my vocabulary probably developed as a result of my love of reading; she often found me curled up with a good book. Honestly, I don't think they believed her. I started reading a lot soon after Sarah died. Perhaps I was looking for an escape from this world, and books offered me that.

Mom was convinced that all that reading made up for my lack of attention in school, and somehow kept me from totally sinking below the academic criterion. I knew what I had to do to get by. I know that sounds pretty lazy, but I assure you, it wasn't laziness. I understood school's importance; I just didn't think it was the *only* important thing in my life. Sandy, riding, racing and the rodeo, those things were just as important to me, maybe even more important.

During those times when I needed to escape my haunting thoughts, I usually turned to books about horses, other animals, and stories about the outdoors. A good book came in handy nearly every day. I particularly liked *The Frontier Boys,* by Glen Balth. Whenever I got a new book, I made sure it was the next one in the series. When I was younger, I read about Roy Rogers and the Lone Ranger. Once I got to high school, I began to read Zane Gray's western novels. My favorite Gray books were *Roping Lions in the Grand Canyon*, and *The Light of Western Stars.*

I told Jonathan that I had a message from Mom. "Mom wanted me to stop in and ask you and Susan to come over for dinner. She's making pot roast tonight, and you know she always makes enough to feed an army."

"Sure, Will, I'll pick Susan up after work and head over." I could tell Jonathan was pleased Mom asked him and Susan to come by. He hadn't been over for dinner in a while, and I'm sure he missed Mom's cooking. Susan admitted she wasn't much of a cook, but Mom said that was all right because she made up for her lack of culinary skills in so many other ways. We were all impressed with how loving and kind she was to Jonathan and the way she doted on Christopher and Lenny as if they were her own children. I had a feeling that Susan was going to be a good mom and a good cook one day too. She had that same love in her heart that I saw in Mom, and Mom always said that was the most important ingredient. Who could argue with that?

Sitting in what was once Dad's office, I told Jonathan, "Great! I think mom could use some extra company around the house tonight. She looked really lost this morning. She's so sad, John. She's obviously trying to be strong for the rest of us, and do all that she can to hide her pain. I wish she didn't feel like she had to do that. At night, when I hear her crying softly for Dad, I usually go sit in the hall outside her door. You probably think I'm weird for doing that. I just don't know what else to do. So, I sit there with my head on my knees, wishing things could be the way they used to be."

"No, Will. I don't think you're weird, I understand completely. I wish the same could be true, but the reality is that Dad's gone, and unfortunately there is nothing we can do about that. All we can do is be here for each other and pray the pain one day will subside for all of us. Tell Mom I'll be there, and I'll be there on time."

Chapter 5
My Rebellious Past

As I walked home, I began to think about my life before Dad died. All I could think about was how disappointing I had once been. I went through a pretty rough time after Sarah died. Something inside me changed. I felt so responsible for what happened to her. I believed it was my fault, and all that guilt began to take over my mind and play serious havoc with my emotions. Mom and Dad tried to convince me that Sarah's death wasn't my fault, but what else could they say? I believed it to be true, and it wasn't long before I was out of control.

During this period of my life, I was a bother, as well as a constant burden for the people in my life that truly cared about me, like my dad. Looking back, I realize how much stress and aggravation I caused my parents.

Many of the people closest to me said that I had a real wild streak, and if I didn't change my ways, my destiny would be jail or death. No bones about it! Suffice it to say, I was a man living a life running from yesterday and refusing to look toward tomorrow.

Now that Dad's gone, I feel even worse about all the trouble I caused for him and everyone else. Self-destructive behavior had become my lifestyle. Unfortunately, Dad felt the need to rescue me most of the time. The guilt of each rescue haunts me and leaves me with a lot of remorse.

I may not have realized it at the time, but fortunately for me, Dad finally had had enough. He decided not to rescue me anymore. If I was ever going to change, I had to feel the pain of my choices, and he knew that. I'm sure it wasn't easy for him to allow me to suffer my own consequences. I could tell it really pained him. More than anything, I knew he wanted to make all my troubles go away, but he could no longer do that. He knew the only way I would ever make better choices was to suffer the pain of their consequence. Not only that, I think he just finally reached a point of exhaustion, and concluded that my rebellion warranted a "hands off" response. God knows he was right!

One of the worst times (when Dad refused to lend a helping hand) was the day I ended up in jail. My 'hot head' and bad temper landed me behind bars for one of the longest nights I will ever remember. It all happened one hot, humid summer night. Chuckie's Restaurant was having an 'all you can eat' clambake. Most of my friends were going to be there, and I was always up for a party. My best friend, Bart Murray and I were standing outside talking with Chuckie. During a break in our conversation, I overheard Dave Ross talking about my sister.

A group of boys discussing Shannon was not uncommon, but the conversation was usually flattering, commendatory and respectful. Wherever Shannon went, she seemed to capture the attention of most gentlemen folk, and as long as they acted like gentlemen, she never really minded. Due to her daily dose of tennis, Shannon was slender and physically strong. She is five foot eight and has always appeared self-confident. Bart, my friend, once described Shannon as "a young woman who could not only get attention but lots of dates as well." Bart claims he said it only to be silly. He called it goofing around; I believed it was a crush, but I never told him that.

Shannon's hair is a natural shade of light flaxen. (She doesn't like the term blond; she thinks it sounds boring. She's a constant reader of those silly romance novels, and I just think all that has really gone to her head.) She is very pretty, extremely smart, and equally as delightful. We're pretty close, and I couldn't ask for a nicer sister.

Much to my father's dismay, she never tried to hide her long legs, wearing shorts and skirts that passed above the knee line. There were quite a few times I remember hearing Dad say, "Shannon march yourself right back up those stairs! Those short skirts might be the trend today, but you're not wearing one! Dress like a young lady for heaven's sake!" Mom and Dad came from an era where a woman's skirt touched her ankle, but girls didn't dress that way anymore. Shannon had never worn a skirt that I thought was too revealing, just shorter than my Dad was used to. It took him quite a while before he could get used to that style.

Recognizing that Shannon may have caused the boys to glance her way from time to time was one thing, but that didn't warrant crude comments, especially coming from the likes of Dave Ross.

On this particular evening, Bart knew right away that I'd overheard something I didn't like. As hot anger started to consume me, Bart began to watch me with that familiar, nervous look; it was the look Bart sometimes got when he knew I was about to do something that could wind us both in a lot of trouble.

"Now wait a minute, Will. Let's try to solve this one without a fight. Dave's a mean 'son of a you know what', and he's not worth your trouble. Come on Will, walk away."

I strongly objected, "Did you hear what he said Bart? Did you hear what he called my sister? You don't think I'm just gonna walk away while he insults her do you? Bart, are you with me or not?"

I could tell that Bart, too, did not appreciate rude comments about Shannon. It was obvious that he had taken an interest in Shannon. Sometimes I caught Bart looking at her in a way a person does only when they have a crush, a kind of dreamy type stare. It was a bit pathetic. Unbeknownst to him, I have always been aware of the way he felt about her, but I have never let on. At the time, I found his infatuation to be a bit fruitless, never believing for one moment that Shannon would go out with him.

"Okay, Will, I can tell by the look in your eyes that I'm not going to convince you otherwise. I've got your back," Bart said with his full support.

I walked up to Dave and got right in his face. "Did I hear you right? Are you talking about my sister?"

Dave didn't care what I said, he just continued to say rude and insensitive things about Shannon, and he dared me to try to do something about it.

"All right, Dave, I will do something about it!" I spoke with absolute certainty and determined reprisal. Before anyone knew it, punches were flying, and crowds of people were pushing and yelling, trying to see the fight.

Dave was now at my mercy, as I had him pinned to the ground teaching him a lesson of my own, when I felt a tap on my shoulder. I didn't even look to see who it was; I just turned around and nailed the guy, right across the jaw. He fell hard to the ground. When I looked at him, I knew there was going to be big trouble. Not only was he an incredibly huge man standing about six feet four, he also happened to be a New York State trooper. Needless to say, I was arrested and was given the honor of spending an extremely long night in jail. Dad could have bailed me out that evening, but he said a night in jail would do me some good. A night in jail was his hope of somehow straightening me out. I wish that was all it took, but it wasn't.

Another one of my crazy ideas took me to nearby Canada. Bart Murray and I often went to Montreal to box for a hundred bucks. It didn't matter how long we lasted in the ring, or whether or not we won; the money was always the same, a hundred bucks. Whatever gave us the 'hare-brained idea' to do such a foolish thing still baffles me today. We were put in the ring with some very big guys that had muscles on top of muscles. The only justification I could reckon was that I must have had a lot of pent up guilt and anger, and I had a need to pound it out of something or somebody. Aside from that, I was just young and stupid, I guess.

The last fight I ever fought in Canada left me quite bruised. When mom saw me the next morning, she was horrified. She had no idea I was even in Canada, let alone fighting in boxing matches.

Crying and yelling, she really let me have it, "What am I going to do with you, Will? I'm so afraid you're going to end up dead somewhere, because you don't have the good sense to use the brain God gave you! I've had it, Will! You're going to have to straighten up or move yourself right out of here! All this worrying about you is causing way too much strain on this family. Before you go doing something dangerous and foolish again, take the time to think about your father

and me and the rest of the people in this house that care about you!"
Mom knew I was living out of my wounds, and she didn't know how to
change that. So, as though her comments were futile, she stormed out
of the room.

There was another time when I had done some farm work for Ray
Brook. Ray wasn't the nicest guy in town. His face was pitted and red,
common with men who drink too much and bellow way too often.
Warning me not to be overly judgmental, Dad said he wasn't always
that way, and there was actually a time when he used to be a pretty nice
guy.

Ray used to be married to a sweet girl named Mildred. They had two
young sons. One day his wife ended up in the hospital, unconscious,
with a severe blow to the head. Ray said she fell down the stairs,
carrying a load of laundry. The stairs Ray was talking about were not
your normal flight of stairs. These were long and steep. Mildred and
Ray had a two-story house, and Ray used the bottom floor for his car
repair shop. Dad said that he used to be the best mechanic in town.

Outside, a long narrow staircase stretched from the ground floor up
to the balcony. The balcony ran across the entire front expanse of their
house. Mildred often took in other people's laundry in order to earn a
little extra money. She used to hang the laundry from a clothesline that
reached from their balcony to a huge maple on the other side of their
property. One day, while carrying a load down the stairs, Mildred
tripped just as her foot hit the second step. That's where her plunge
began. At the bottom of the stairs, she collided with the ground, and
there she lay unconscious, unconsciousness she never recovered from.
Within four days of the fall, Ray laid Mildred to rest in St. John's
cemetery, which is only a stone throw from his home.

Ray and the boys were devastated. Life at the Brook house was
never the same. Eventually the boys got married and left home. One
moved to Saratoga and the other to Rochester. The boys and their
families don't make it home very often. Tragic and sad, a family that
was once blissful and secure seems forever broken apart.

Losing Mildred left Ray unhappy and inconsolable. Alcohol

became Ray's medication, and it soon changed him. Sadly, he became an angry, miserable, wretchedly mean rogue brute!

Hanging out in the bars didn't render 'Mr. Rogue Ray' with an assortment of very good friends. There didn't seem to be a soul in Ray's life trying to help him get his life back on track. If you ask me, I think Ray was intentionally ruining his life. He simply lost the passion for life and living, and his tomorrows just didn't matter to him anymore. I understood this kind of thinking, and I think if it weren't for my family, I could have ended up just like Ray.

Word around town was that Ray was looking for someone to come to his home and do a bit of work for him. When Ray asked me if I was interested, I was hesitant, but I wanted the money, so I agreed. My job description involved mowing his lawn, moving hay onto a tractor bed, and doing various odd jobs around the house. He said it shouldn't take me more than a week to get everything done.

Once each job was explained to me, I was told that I would get paid on Friday. After a bit of negotiating, we shook hands. Dad always told me that a handshake is a man's bond. In spite of Ray's reputation, I trusted him. It doesn't matter who I'm working for or what job I'm doing, I work hard. I spared no less for Ray Brook.

On Friday, I went looking for Ray to get paid. I found him down town in Chuckie's Restaurant. He was talking to one of the 'regulars' when I walked in.

I introduced myself to the lady he was talking to and asked if I could please speak to Ray for a moment. He looked at me, put his hand on my chest, and gave me a shove. He told me to get lost! He knew I was looking to get paid. He said he'd pay me when he felt like it, and right then, he didn't feel like it! "Can't you see that I'm busy here, boy? Get lost!"

Maybe I should have felt sorry for Ray, and cut him some slack, but like I said, my heart was pretty hard at this juncture in my life. That simply wasn't a time when I was making very good choices, and in the forefront of my mind there was no way I was going to let Ray Brook embarrass me like that! All I knew was that my temper was raging, and

I had to do something to get even with that mean, hateful, old brute of a man.

I headed back to his farm and picked up the hay wagon full of freshly cut hay. Driving to the iron bridge that sits right in the middle of town, I unhitched it. With a flick of a match, I set the thing ablaze and watched the whole thing go up in smoke. Ray could never prove that I did it, but he learned that day that I was not just some kid he could push around. He never did pay me, but watching his face as his wagon burned to the ground, leaving only ashes, was payment enough for me. Ray Brook got what he deserved; that was the only care in my mind at that time.

Little did I know that the burning wagon set into motion something that would forever change my life and in a most extraordinary way. Dad knew that I was the one who had burned the hay wagon. He told Mom that he was really worried about me, and that he had tried everything he knew to get me to straighten up. As strange as it sounds, Mom suggested a horse. She knew there was a time in Dad's life when horses seemed to be the only thing that gave him any solace. She told Dad that maybe I just needed something like that. Something to not only keep me busy, but also something to take care of, to enjoy, and possibly to even love. A horse would keep me busy and hopefully teach me some responsibility. Both of my parents knew how much I loved animals, so Mom convinced Dad that a horse of my own might teach me some responsibility and probably make me happy as well. She was right. Once Dad introduced me to Sandy, my life was never the same. As sure as the day is long, I knew Sandy helped save me from a life of ruin.

Chapter 6
Dad's Past Revealed

Mom had planned a big meal, and she wanted the entire family to be there. Jonathan and Susan showed up around six thirty. Shannon, Lenny and Christopher were already in the house, and I came in from the barn. The house was filled with delicious aromas, and the large pot roast baking in the oven smelled wonderfully appetizing.

Mom had a way of trying to make cooking and eating a celebration. She has even been known to use her cooking as a possible remedy for a problem. Even when nothing in my life seemed the same anymore, mom's cooking had a way of putting the floor beneath my feet. I have to say that the memories I recalled when walking into our kitchen were a confusing mixture of anticipation and sadness. I was glad we could all be together during dinner, but there was also that unmistakable void. I'm sure we were all thinking about Dad and wishing he was with us. It seemed his absence was even more intolerable around mealtime.

When Sarah left us, I showed very little appreciation for my family, but thankfully (due to an unconventional antidote named Sandy and caring parents) I've grown since then. It was very comforting to have Jonathan and Susan around, as well as Shannon and the boys. Rather than fighting their sincerity and loyalty, I was learning to embrace it in my own quiet way.

Shannon had been sitting in Dad's favorite chair, reading a novel by William Gibson, called *The Miracle Worker*. You could often find a good book on her lap. That is one thing Shannon and I have in common; we both really love to read. The only difference is that she loves romance with a bit of mystery, and I love books about the Wild West and animals, especially horses.

There was a familiar and comforting scent found on Dad's chair where Shannon was often found reading. The fragrant and unique combination of cologne, sawdust, and motor oil brought back fond remembrances of Dad. It's true what they say; smell is the most powerful of the five senses when it comes to conjuring up memories. So often, I too sat in Dad's chair to read. But ever since my dad passed away, I seemed to have lost my interest in reading. Whenever I did take the time to sit in Dad's chair, I sat quietly with my eyes closed, breathing in deeply the memory of the man I missed so much. I would try to remember his smile, his laugh and the funny jokes he used to tell. Oh, man, his jokes sure were funny. Some of his yarns were told to teach, some to make us think, but mostly he told them just to make us laugh.

As sad as it makes me feel, I have always enjoyed reflecting back, remembering how smart Dad was. While helping me to straighten out my life, not once did he treat me like a child, but as a man. Dad believed that if he treated me like a grownup, I would more likely act like one. He was right.

Mom was in the kitchen checking the roast and stirring one of the pots on the stovetop. She always timed things so each food was finished at the same time. Susan said that took talent. She said that when she cooks, something is always getting cold while something else is still cooking. Mom has always made it look so easy, so I never realized cooking could be so complicated.

"Mom, what can I do to help?" asked Shannon.

"Oh thanks Shannon, I could really use your help. Would you please set the table?"

"Sure, Mom." Shannon's tone was almost always pleasant when speaking with our mom. Mom and Shannon got along incredibly well. Some people say that when a girl gets to be Shannon's age, she can become trouble. Trying to be 'all independent' can make them a bit rebellious. This never happened to Shannon. I think it's because I created enough rebellion for the entire family, and she saw how much it hurt my parents.

Being the only girl, she had a great deal in common with Mom. They both enjoyed cooking, and believe it or not, they loved to clean. They said it gave them a sense of order and comfort in their lives. I remember the day I asked Shannon why she liked to clean. (I thought she was crazy to like such a thing.)

She responded, "All I can tell you, Will, is that when my life is clean and organized, I feel better. When it's not, I can get real moody."

I said to myself, *Oh yeah, I remember those moody moments!*

Mom's reason for cleaning was more on the spiritual side. She's always said that, "God's a God of order, and I'm smart enough to listen to Him."

Lenny and Christopher had been in the front room watching *Dennis the Menace*, their favorite show. Maybe they have watched that sitcom too often. Let's just say, that Dennis kid and my two little brothers have way too much in common. Some of their antics could have been learned from good ol' Dennis, like the time they dug up Mrs. Bailey's butterfly bush and perennial lilies to bring home to Mom. They told Mom that flowers grow when you're nice and you talk to them, and that Mrs. Bailey was way too grumpy to grow pretty flowers. Oh boy, they got in trouble that day!

Mom began putting the dinner into serving dishes. "You boys go get washed up for dinner!" she called. As usual, the boy's just sat there, glued to the TV. "Christopher and Lenny, unless you want a spanking across your backside, I suggest you hit the off switch and get your 'behinds' to the bathroom!"

All mom ever had to do was mention the word spanking and those boys moved lickety-split. It wasn't very often that she resorted to corporal punishment, but if she found it necessary, you can be sure Mom would. Discipline, was usually handed out by Mom, rarely by Dad. Most of the time, Dad was very mild mannered. Nearly every aspect of his personality radiated gentleness; so, we absolutely hated it if we did upset him. It seemed that Dad only got worked up by our behavior about once a year. We then knew we had gone too far. We held our breaths, waiting for that otherwise, pleasant man to return. Within a few minutes, Dad was calm and even a bit regretful that he had lost his temper. Some punishments might then be calmly meted out.

Mom never liked the TV. The 'devil box', as she referred to it, was having an influence not only on Lenny and Christopher, but on lots of other kids as well. In her mind, it interfered with school performance, roused disrespect for authority, and most certainly took away from family conversational time. Not to mention that one of her favorite enjoyments, the radio, was becoming a thing of the past.

While we were at school, Mom would get a jump start on preparing dinner. While cooking, she would listen to her treasured ivory Plaskon radio with its glowing red dial and ivory knobs. Mom tuned in to listen to big band music. She would tell us about the good old days when she would listen to all of the "wonderful" radio programs. *Life of Riley* was one of her favorites. Hilarious was how she described it. This character, Riley, didn't have a mean bone in his body, but unfortunately not much of a brain either. He was always finding himself in a heap of trouble, and it was these troubled moments that Mom said were so funny. Dad enjoyed listening to *Gun Smoke*.

The empty chair where Dad once sat didn't go unnoticed; yet, not a word was spoken about it. Once each of us was seated at the table, Mom asked if I would like to say grace. Our Dad had always been the one to say grace, so I tried to remember some of the ways he used to say it.

I told Mom that I would do my best. "Dear Heavenly Father, bless this food we share tonight, and bless the loving hands that prepared it. May our meal together be spent remembering days gone by along with the current reflections of today. Give each of us strength in our sadness as we remember Dad and the times we shared. Your Word says, 'Apart from the body; present with the Lord.' We are so thankful that Dad was a man of prayer and a man of faith. We know he is there with You in heaven, and we will see him again," and then with the sign of the cross, "In the name of the Father, Son and Holy Spirit. Amen."

"That was really nice, Will. You would have made your Dad very proud. In fact, I think you did make him proud. I don't believe he is as far off as we often think he is. There is not a day that goes by that I don't feel his presence," said Mom.

Shannon had the look of pure understanding after Mom spoke. "I think you're right, Mom. I feel like Dad's here a lot of the time too."

I wish I could have known that same feeling, but I didn't. All I felt was loneliness and a great emptiness.

My perplexed face caused Jonathan to quickly speak. My assumption is that he felt as I did. "Well, I do know one thing; Dad would have loved this meal. Mom, this looks great! Susan and I are going to have to come here more often!"

With her lips lightly pressed together and slightly turned up at the corners, she looked at Jonathan with love and gratitude. "You are always welcome here."

"Thanks, Mom," Jonathan replied.

Looking at Mom I could see she had something on her mind. I didn't know it at the time, but she was trying to think of a way to broach the subject of Dad's past.

Mustering the nerve, Mom began to speak. "Kids, I wanted you all to be here tonight, because I have something I want to share with you. I know these past few months have been really difficult and very painful. Being without your father is never going to be easy. Sometimes the best way to heal is to talk about what you are feeling. Exchanging feelings was never easy for your father. Many of his memories were kept hidden, fearing their exposure might deepen his wounds. Your father never spoke about his parents, your grandparents, because their memory made him feel rejected all over again and very sad. Unfortunately, he not only suffered grief, but abandonment as well. By sharing with you more about your dad and his past, I am hoping the heaviness you feel will lessen. Rather than feeling so far removed from him, the closeness you long to experience again will return in a different, yet very special way."

Jonathan spoke up, "What did happen to Dad's parents, our grandfather and grandmother? Why did he feel rejected by them?"

Mom began her rendition of the past, "You're grandmother's name was Molly and your grandfather's name was Harry. Your dad was named after him."

"I never even knew his name, let alone that Dad was named after him." said Lenny.

Mom continued, "Your grandparents were entertainers. They performed in a vaudeville act, known as the Little Miss Molly and Harry Show."

"What kind of act did they do?" Susan asked.

" ll their act was pretty wide-ranging. They did a lot of dancing they also performed some comedy acts.

an understatement when you looked at Christopher. t all sounds kinda weird to me."

herself, Mom put Christopher at ease. "Someday again when you are a little bit older. Maybe all you need to know right now is that Vaudeville is about singing, dancing and funny jokes."

"Maybe that's why Dad could tell so many funny jokes. He had really funny jokes!" Lenny shouted.

With a pleased look upon her face, Mom said that she thought Lenny was absolutely right. Explaining a bit more, Mom continued, "Molly and Harry became friends with people like Mae West and Red Buttons. Their act had really hit the big time. During their peek of success, Molly found out she was pregnant. Unfortunately, Molly never wanted children. Her career was the most important thing in her life, and she never wanted that to change, especially now that her career was really taking off. A baby would take her away from her dream, a life that she and Harry lived and died for."

Claire paused for a moment, as if to try and understand the mindset of Molly, to no avail she continued on. "Becoming a mommy to this child was not a part of her plans. She was very much like a child herself. Given her self-centered nature, Harry had all he could do to keep Molly from some destructive behaviors. Disappointments often sent Molly into a rage. This often resulted in very unpleasant scenes. Molly's shrill voice could be heard for extended periods of time and by all within shouting range."

Mom interrupted her story to tell Lenny and Christopher that it was time to get ready for bed. She said she would be up in a little while to tuck them in and say their prayers. The boys seemed a bit relieved; the story was becoming too difficult for them to follow. And I was relieved as well. I could tell this conversation was getting a bit too deep for Christopher and Lenny to fully grasp. Once the boys were gone, and Mom picked up where she had left off, I had an even better understanding of why she wanted the boys to leave the room.

"During the last four months of her pregnancy, Molly could no longer perform on stage. At this point in Molly's career, her act had become a bit racy and possibly even a bit daring. Harry and Molly were a talented singing duo, who could dance and sing like nobody's business. They both were also skillful comedians who were more than adept at making people laugh, much too talented to resort to such daring performances. Living the life of Vaudville, a performer had to contend with the pressures and influences that often came with it. Some could endure and pass by the evils sometimes associated with the 'glitz and glam', but Molly and Harry were never able." Mom took a moment to examine the expressions on our faces, realizing she had shared with us some coarse particulars relating to our family heritage.

We urged her to continue, and Mom went on. "Later, a letter had been found written by Harry; he expressed his hope that when Molly left to spend her last trimester at home, she would somehow bond with the child growing inside her. Instead, Molly became more and more resentful, hating her predicament. Sadly, Harry was unable to quiet her rancor and help her accept the inevitability of motherhood. She was inconsolable.

"On what I would refer to as an eventful evening, when the thermometer read twenty degrees below zero, with a wind chill factor of negative fifty degrees, and a report of another Nor'easter heading our way, God decided it was time for Molly to go into labor. Our North Country has always been known for its extreme winters, and this particular winter was no exception. Despite the blizzard-like conditions, Dr. Swartz was asked to make a house call to the Casey home. Staying with Harry's parents at the time was part of Molly's plan. She never wanted any of her Vaudeville friends to know she was pregnant, so Harry agreed to move up north until the baby was born.

"Harry's mom, May, was a beautiful person inside and out. She so much wanted Molly and Harry to give up their crazy life of thirsting for stardom, and trade it in for a more stable life, especially now that a child was on the way. She tried unsuccessfully to convince Molly that her ~~child~~ was a gift from God, a blessing. May was shocked when Molly ~~no~~ blessing, but rather a curse. Once those words ~~frightened~~ for her. Molly was ~~telling~~ her

cried like ~~the~~

"Molly held him for a short ~~while~~ peculiar way. May said that she couldn't tell if Molly ~~was~~ second thoughts, imagining a life with this adorable child, or if her face was expressing resentment. As it turned out, Molly and Harry left a week later, leaving your dad behind with May. Thank God for his grandparents, May and William. They gave him lots of love and tried to fill the void left by his parents. Molly and Harry returned only once or twice a year. It was then that they put on a show for the locals."

We were all dumbfounded! What kind of people would give up their child for something so pathetic, so vain? It was difficult to believe that Dad's parents could abandon him like that.

How could this generation before me be so cold and unfeeling, especially people who shared a heredity with my dad? Dad was the farthest thing from cold. He loved us and would have sacrificed everything for us.

I decided to say something, since no one else had yet spoken. "No wonder Dad never wanted to talk about his parents. Dad may be gone, but at least we have many incredibly happy and positive memories to remember him by. Being loved and wanted by his parents was never part of Dad's childhood memory. He must have felt so empty. Please tell me he didn't somehow feel unworthy because they did that to him. Did Dad ever tell you how all of this made him feel?"

With all seriousness, Mom began to explain. "Will, he only spoke of this once, and that was just before we introduced you to Sandy. He wanted so much for you to have a good life. He was so worried you would throw away the gift of a loving family, as well as every other good thing you have been given. You were in jeopardy of losing everything, possibly even your life, because you couldn't or wouldn't get that rebellious and discontented spirit from your soul. Dad always believed you were a gentle, kind, loving person with admirable convictions; but, he was so worried that after Sarah died, your guilt and grief would cause such self-hatred within you that it would destroy you. Rebellion and self-centeredness was at the core of his mother's personality, while weakness and blind devotion to Molly seemed to dominate his father's character. Terrible guilt and a false sense of responsibility haunted him, believing that somehow it was his fault you had this dangerous, wild streak. He feared it was a trait that you were predisposed to, planted by a generational seed. Your father prayed daily that you would be set free from your destructive behavior."

Mom reached over and placed her hand on mine. "Your Dad believed Sandy would provide hope for you. He could see himself in you and knew that Sandy could become, in time, an anchor of stability you desperately needed. As you rode him, spent time with him, and eventually learned to love him like a friend, he believed, with all his heart that you would change. It was his hope that Sandy would teach you about caring, responsibility and gentleness."

Deeply touched by all that my mom said, I had one question, "How did Dad know Sandy could accomplish so much?"

With certainty she said, "Because it took a horse, by the name of Jackson, to help give meaning to your Dad's life. Rejection caused your dad to act in a most reckless manner. Due to a praying grandmother, I believe, Harry was saved from utter destruction. Your great grandfather William gave Jackson to your dad, hoping it would give Harry something to look forward to each day. And, Will, one of the

58

most interesting parts of your dad's story is that Sandy is part of Jackson's lineage. Jackson lived three generations before Sandy. And there is something else you need to know. It was important to your dad that Jackson and Sandy's lineage continue. Sandy sired two foals coming to our place."

it! Jackson became exactly what Dad needed, just there were two horses that closer to

Chapter 7
What About Sandy?

As I lay in my bed, the clock read 12:35. I was very tired, but I couldn't sleep. Thoughts were racing around in my head as I wrestled with a very important decision. The time had come for me to make the critical choice as to whether or not I would continue racing. Riding and racing had always been something Dad and I shared together. I honestly didn't know if there was an ounce of my being that desired to race again. Each time I thought about getting on the back of a horse, I was reminded, ever so clearly, that Dad was gone.

While contemplating my future, an unexpected thought came to me. What about Sandy? If I chose to no longer race, how would that affect him? Not only did I have a dream and a passion for the race, so did Sandy. Without a doubt, I knew that I could wallow in my anger, sorrow and self-pity for a very long time. Without Dad, racing and life in general had lost a lot of its purpose and allure. I believed I could give up racing right then and there, but could Sandy? Why had I been so selfish? I hadn't even thought of Sandy and how my decision would affect him! Without a challenge, without that race to the finish, I knew Sandy would lose his zest for life. The thought of depriving Sandy of his passion caused me to rethink my future.

anything to have him there by my side, but that morning, I felt something akin to what Mom had talked about. I sensed a soothing touch, a bit of warmth in the midst of my sadness. It was a feeling of closeness, a sense of inner strength. The peace I had about my decision to race again truly surpassed my understanding. It was as if I knew that Dad would want me to look forward, not backward.

If I chose to look back, I would look back with fond memories of all that Dad and I shared. The love of horses and racing had belonged to us. I felt blessed that it provided a connection that most fathers and sons only dream of experiencing. With each practice race, I remembered all the helpful instruction and advice Dad gave. "Don't hold the reins too tightly; let Sandy lead; work to the inside." Dad's voice was whispering in my head. At will, I was able to hear and feel Dad's presence.

Sandy and I began training for the Grand Championship Quarter-Horse Race that was to be held in August. Since I made the decision to continue racing, it seemed only right to dedicate any racing success to my dad. It became clear that I could dwell on Dad not being there, or I could race in his honor. I chose the latter.

After our morning run, I brushed Sandy down and set things in order for his day. I made sure he had all he needed to eat, and drink, and then I contacted Gregg Pace, our close family friend, to see if he would stop by and work with Sandy a bit. Gregg Pace had been one of Dad's best friends. They met many years ago when Dad was racing quarter horses in Kateyville. Often, while racing, he observed a man keenly watching him and his horse, Jackson. Finally one day, Dad decided to approach the guy and inquire about his obvious curiosity. He learned that Gregg Pace was a well-respected horse trainer. He helped train some of the most famous horses of his time. Captivated by his knowledge and expertise, Dad was elated to learn that Jackson reminded him of one particular quarter horse he had the privilege of training, a "King-bred" horse by the name of Hosea. It was then that Dad learned exactly what it meant to be a "King-bred" horse.

That day, Gregg Pace shared with Dad the story of a man by the name of Jess Hankin who owned a famous horse called King. His horse was known as being the "Cornerstone of the quarter-horse industry". King was responsible for producing quarter-horse colts that eventually exceeded all expectations and excelled in the world of racing. These horses made him the most famous sire of the horse-breeding world. On March 24, 1958, twenty-six year old King died of a heart attack, but before his passing, he produced 520 registered colts. One of these foals was Hosea. Hosea was trained by Mr. Pace and went on to win several grand championships on a professional circuit. Not only had Hosea been an unbeatable racing horse, he also had a gentle temperament that contrasted with many of the thoroughbreds around him. Hosea inherited many of King's innate qualities. King remained a formidable racer and a gentle sole right up to his death and Hosea did as well. Dad was amazed and thrilled to learn Jackson had been compared to such racing legends.

If I was going to continue racing, there was someone I needed to call, Gregg Pace. Gregg was the one person, other than Dad, who would understand the challenge that Sandy and I faced. Progress could still be made to improve our speed and strategy. Sandy listened instinctively to three people: Dad, Gregg and me. Now that Dad was gone, I

Chapter 9
Who's That Girl?

Sitting at our usual spot in the lunchroom, I shared with Bart the productive morning I had with Gregg and Sandy. "Sandy amazes me, Bart. He gets faster every day. You watch; we're gonna win this year's Grand Championship, and win it big!"

With an agreeable tone, Bart replied, "No doubt, Will. You two are the best this race has to offer. Who knows, maybe this is just the beginning for you two. Maybe after you graduate, you and Sandy can compete professionally."

I was surprised Bart mentioned that. Deep in my heart, I knew that I wanted to race professionally some day. "I thought about that very thing, Bart. I just didn't want to say it out loud; I worried I might jinx myself or something."

Bart chuckled, "Oh come on; you don't believe in all that stuff, do you?"

"Not really, but I just want to be careful. I don't want to get my hopes up and then be disappointed."

As Bart looked up, he saw the Bailey twins coming toward them. "Watch out, Will, you're about to get bombarded. The Bailey twins are coming. They want you bad, man!" Bart chided.

I tried to slouch down in my seat so as not to be seen, but it was to no avail. With her tiny, high-pitched voice, Barbara Bailey began to speak. "Hi, Will. Are you going to the sock hop tonight? I'd sure like it if you saved a dance for me."

I responded. "Oh, hey Barb! Um, I don't know if I'm going or not.

I don't really like to dance. I think Bart and I are just going to hang out at my house and ride the horses a bit. But thanks for asking."

Cindy Bailey chimed in, "Oh, come on Will, don't you do anything else other than ride that horse of yours? You need to get out and have some fun!"

Bart decided to make me sweat a little bit by leading the girls on. "I don't know, girls. Maybe we'll stop by, but you won't catch eith dancing. Will and I don't dance; we just listen to the music. And I know if you know this or not, but that great music you will be lister to tonight, just happens to be my brother's band. Will and I are helpi him get set up tonight before the hop. Stop by then, and I will introduce you girls to the guys in the band."

With gleeful anticipation, the girls responded, "Groovy Bart! We'll be there! See ya tonight!"

I glared at Bart; I couldn't believe he had invited the Bailey twins to the gym before the sock hop even began. "What are you doing, Bart! We're going to be stuck with them all night. You know they won't leave us alone. You just gave live bait to two man-eating sharks, for goodness sake!"

"Oh, lighten up, Will," Bart responded.

"Once they meet the guys in the band, you and I will be a distant memory. You'll see; trust me."

I told Bart that if he was wrong, I was going to make him pay, and when I did, it would be absolutely no fun for him, no fun at all!

On Friday, the school day certainly dragged on. I couldn't wait to get out and take my usual run home. The final bell rang, and I was up and out of my seat, speeding toward home. Cayey Lane had been bustling with lots of activity. On Friday night, this little Adirondack town became remarkably alive.

As usual, I passed all the local businesses, but, unlike this past year's qualifying race day, there was no fanfare. I was sure August would tell a different story. On the day of the Grand Championship, I had a strong feeling that this street would be bustling and hopping with cheering and mighty shouts of encouragement. The people here loved a good race. The racetrack usually became a meeting ground for friends and family, a fine excuse just to get together, and a good reason for a person to be able to ignore the stresses of one's typical day. The races also brought wanted patronage to several of the businesses located in Kateyville, boosting the economy for our small town. Lastly, when one of their own was doing well enough to place in a championship race, it gave the people here a sense of pride. All around, it gave excitement to our otherwise sleepy little town.

Sandy was in the barn, patiently awaiting my arrival. As my footsteps were heard, Sandy began to whinny. He was always happy to see me.

I ran into the barn, "Hey boy, how are ya? Let's get you outa here. How does a ride down to the river sound?"

Before long, Sandy and I stood on the banks of the Raquette River. The river was rough as the winds forced white caps to form on the water's surface. Standing there with Sandy, I felt a freeing up within me. I bent down and placed my head upon Sandy's. I loved these special moments spent together, just him and me. Sandy was my best friend and I couldn't imagine a single day without him. Our walk only lasted about an hour. If I hadn't promised Bart I would be at the gym by six o'clock, Sandy and I would have stayed out much longer.

Mom prepared another delicious meal. The appetizing smells barely made it to my nose before I devoured the food on my plate. Part of the pleasure of such a great dinner was enjoying its aroma, but today, I didn't have time for such indulgences.

As soon as I finished eating, I jumped into the shower and then quickly changed my clothes for the sock hop. Vanity had never been one of my character flaws. I didn't put a lot of thought into which shirt I should wear. I chose my most comfortable shirt, even though it had been wadded in a ball and stuffed behind the nightstand. I would have left the house dressed like that if Mom hadn't demanded I change or let her iron it. I opted for a quick change and then hurried off to the school gym.

Bart was waiting on the steps outside the school. "Hey Will, David's band is ready for us to start setting up. Are you set to go?"

"Yup, lead the way." I said.

The Mustang Riders were the name of David's band. Just about anyone who listened to them said the same thing, that they were star material. We thought they could most definitely hold their own against any popular artist within the music world. Yet, the only gigs they were able to get so far were the high school dances in and around Kateyville. Bart truly believed that their time would come. The Mustang Riders would 'hit it big'; he was sure of it. The junior class of Kateyville had hired the band to play at this year's sock hop. They were ecstatic when Bart's brother said they'd play!

Even though Friday night was shaping up to be a hip hoppin' good time, I really wanted no part of it. I told Bart I would help set up, and then I wanted to get home. Sandy and I had an early appointment planned with Gregg, and I wanted to be well rested and ready.

Before the hop began at eight o'clock, the 'Brains', as I called them, of the junior class showed up early to decorate the gym. Hanging out with the 'Brains' had never been my style or idea of fun. I had nothing against them, but I just figured we wouldn't have much in common. I was sure that their idea of fun couldn't possibly include me either. But, as I looked across the room, I began to hope I was wrong. Hanging the traditional junior, sock hop banner was a girl I had never noticed before, and certainly didn't recall seeing at school. From a distance, I could tell she was only about five feet tall, and couldn't weigh more than a hundred pounds. She had subtle blond, long curly hair, tied back neatly into a ponytail. She was wearing a soft pink sweater and cropped jeans rolled with a cuff at the bottom. Barely able to reach the banner, she stood as high as she could on the tips of her toes. As I looked at the bottoms of her clean, white tennis shoes, I could hardly see a spot of dirt beneath her treads. Looking down at my own shoes, I could see a stark contrast. As I did, a familiar thought came to me; I was sure that a 'Brain' would have nothing to do with me.

Gazing now for at least a minute more, I was interrupted by Bart. "Will, help me with this speaker. It's way too heavy for me to lift by myself. Come on! What are you doing?"

I expressed a half-hearted apology to Bart.

Curiosity got the best of Bart, "Who are you lookin' at? If it's a 'Brain', give it up. It's not going to happen."

As if I was faced with a dare, I spoke out, "I don't know, Bart; I think I have to at least find out her name. Don't you think so?"

Bart asked, "Whose name?"

"That cute girl hanging the banner with good ol' 'Dean the Dictionary', who is she?" I queried. "I've never seen her at school."

"That's Lori Dune," said Bart. "She just moved here last week. She's in my math class. Mr. Hennessey introduced her to us on Tuesday. Her dad's in the military or something."

Sarcastically, I countered, "Oh, I forgot; you take math with the 'Brains'."

"Hey, everybody's gotta be good at something- for you, it's racing horses, and for me, it's square roots," Bart rejoined.

I let Bart know that I was just 'pulling his chain'. "Ease up, okay? " I said. "I'm gonna go say hello and introduce myself to her. I'm not afraid of anybody, Bart, let alone a pretty girl who just happens to be of the genius type."

Bart was quick to reply that I had too many girls chasing me now. He was surprised that none of them interested me. Bart had to warn me. "You've always been crazy, Will, and fear certainly isn't one of your attributes. Go for it! I look forward to seeing you get shot down. This will be fun!" Bart said all this with a teasing laugh.

I sarcastically thanked Bart for the confidence he had in me. I told him I wouldn't forget it.

With all the poise I could muster, I approached Lori Dune. "Hi, my name is Will. I heard you're new here at school."

This adorable girl turned around and gave me a peculiar look. She peered over black, cat-eyed glasses. Pushing her spectacles to the tip of her nose, she said, "Hi." She then turned right back around and continued her work.

I had come this far; I couldn't give up now, "I hear your dad is in the military. What branch?"

With what sounded like a warning, Lori said her dad was a major in the Marine Corps. I asked her if she was always this talkative, hoping she didn't mind my sarcasm. She explained that she was sorry if she seemed rude, but that she had a lot to do.

I excused myself and walked away, realizing that learning about Lori Dune was not going to be easy. I knew that there was something special about this girl; she certainly had captivated my attention. She was pretty, smart, and rather unimpressed with me.

"Ouch!" said Bart as he walked up to me. He observed that things hadn't gone so well, and Lori didn't look too interested. Bart told me that I should stick to racing. I didn't find his comments to be very funny. At this point, I just wanted to finish our work and get out of there. Once we finished, I suggested we go get a soda. Bart told me I was reading his mind. We made a 'bee line' for Kuno's Soda Shop.

Chapter 10
The Rodeo

At our Oktoberfest this year, the Rodeo was going to be the exemplar event, and I couldn't wait. Along with racing, I loved the Rodeo! Gregg suggested I not participate in the bareback riding event since the opportunity for injury was too great. I reluctantly complied. As much fun as I had bareback riding, I knew I had to put the Grand Championship race first on my priority list. Besides, competing in several of the other events was going to be a blast! One of my favorites, due to Sandy's keen agility and alertness, was the barrel race. In order to win, Sandy would have to ride against the clock and stay close enough to the barrels without knocking them over. Speed was definitely Sandy's friend, but so was his body awareness. He had an uncanny awareness of how close he was to the barrels.

With three barrels placed one hundred feet apart, Sandy and I had to complete a cloverleaf pattern in the quickest time. Any other pattern would disqualify us immediately. If any barrels were knocked over, that went against our score. Once we rounded the third barrel, Sandy had to race to the finish line. Our official time would be recorded. Sandy seemed to love this contest as much as I did.

Every year when Sandy and I ran the barrel race, Mom stitched a real fancy western outfit for me and made coordinating leg wraps for Sandy. At the Oktoberfest we were fully clad in red, white and blue, a most American look. On my head, was Dad's hat, and pinned to it was Sarah's rose pin and a gold medal that Dad won during the 1936

Kateyville Oktoberfest Barrel Race. The theme of that year's Oktoberfest was, *What the Olympics Should be About.*

That year, the 1936 Olympics were held in Berlin, Germany. The Games of the XI Olympiad were awarded to Germany before the Nazi Party took over the country, but once they came into power, protest erupted around the world. The United States was no exception. But because our country conceded to compete anyway, many Americans were outraged. Kateyville wanted to show its disappointment and disgust at the United State's apparent 'caving'; so, they decided to celebrate the Olympics and the American athlete at home by hosting an event in their honor. Each Rodeo event was awarded either a Bronze, Silver or Gold medal. Dad and his spirited horse, Jackson, gave a precise and superb performance and won a gold medal for their execution of the barrel race.

Dad took the gold in barrel racing, and then received the gold for bull riding. While riding as the header in the team roping competition, Dad, and a close friend named Todd Warner, took the silver. Todd, the heeler, attempted to rope the steer's hind legs. If the heeler only catches one foot, the team is given a five-second penalty. That's exactly what happened, and as a result, another team took the gold. They had to settle for the silver. Mom said that it appeared to her that Dad's God-given talent in rodeo events was generously passed on to me. I was flattered she would say such a thing, and if Mom is indeed correct, I'm surely grateful.

It's interesting that when certain things are said, or I'm in a certain place, or I smell a familiar scent, I begin to think of Sarah. When Mom said I reminded her of Dad, I wondered if Sarah would have liked horses. Maybe she was blessed with Dad's talent as well, and maybe we would have shared a love of horses together. It haunts me with terrible regret that I will never know.

This year's Oktoberfest would host all kinds of events, making it the best one yet. Make no mistake, the Kateyville Rodeo was the best event at each year's Oktoberfest, but several other things would be going on as well. Three bands would be playing, including The Mustang Riders. The bands would kick off the event and play again on Sunday evening to bring the festivities to a close. Games, rides, food venders, and a petting zoo provided a host of activities and lots of fun for the young and the old.

A huge parade, featuring our high school band and majorettes, was set to begin early Saturday morning. It was important that I get to the rodeo track long before the band began their march. Once the parade began and until they finally finished, Cayey Lane would be closed off.

I was really looking forward to the rodeo. It had been a long time since I was able to compete, just for the fun of it. Letting loose and enjoying myself was my only plan, but interestingly enough, fate had a different plan.

Chapter 11
Do You Remember Me?

Saturday morning arrived, and by eight a.m. I was standing in the Rodeo Circle. I decided to stroll the grounds in an effort to walk off some of the jitters that I was beginning to feel. Every year I employed the same routine. I grabbed Sandy's reigns and we walked the entire fair grounds, checking out every ride, exhibit, game, and food vender. The Kateyville Oktoberfest offered about one hundred concession-aires. We had become the biggest Rodeo attraction north of Albany, and Kateyville was real proud of that accomplishment.

As Sandy and I were walking, I spotted Lori Dune sitting outside a Marine Recruitment booth. I told Sandy we shouldn't be rude, that we must say hello. Lori was sitting in a lawn chair reading a book. As I approached, she never even lifted her head. She was completely immersed in her novel.

"Hi, Lori. Do you remember me? I spoke to you at the school the other night," I stammered.

Lori looked up at me, examined me for a bit and then replied, "I believe your name is Will. Am I right?"

"You sure are! This is my horse, Sandy." Thank God, she remembered me! It was certainly possible that she wouldn't recall who I was at all, given her disinterest in me the last time we spoke.

Lori's eyes gleamed as she reached up to pet Sandy on the nose. "Well, hello, Sandy. It's very nice to meet you."

"So, what brings you to the Oktoberfest this year, Lori? Wait a minute. Don't tell me. I'll bet it's your Dad." I hoped I didn't sound completely senseless. For some reason, this girl made me stumble over my words. This had never happened to me before; so, I didn't know how to calm myself down.

Lori didn't seem to notice my uneasiness and began explaining what her dad was doing. "Yes, my Dad is here in Kateyville to set up a new recruitment center. During the Oktoberfest, he's presenting and explaining to the town what the recruitment center is going to be like, and why the government wants it here. The center will open next week on Cayey Lane. It will be located in the vacant building beside Leslie's Beauty Shop."

As she spoke, I wondered how long she and her dad would be stationed here. "Well, that's pretty neat. I hope everything goes well for him. I hope he has fun." There I go, saying something half-witted again.

"Thanks, Will, but I'm sure everything will be fine," Lori answered.

"Would you like to come and see Sandy and me perform in the Rodeo today?" I asked, hoping she would agree.

"I may be able to watch. I'm not sure if my Dad is going to need me today," she responded honestly.

I replied, "Okay, fair enough; but, just so you have all the details, the Rodeo starts at eleven o'clock. The first event is the barrel race, and this just happens to be Sandy's favorite. I'm sure he would love it if you came to see him. Wouldn't you, Sandy?"

Sandy gave a neigh and a nod as if to say, yes! Lori and I both thought that was pretty funny. Each of us gave a quick laugh as I winked at Sandy.

"Thanks for the invitation, Will. You too, Sandy. I will try to make it." Lori replied with a bit more interest than she displayed earlier.

I responded with a bit more confidence and hope. "Great, Lori. We'll keep an eye out for you."

As Sandy and I walked away, my heart was doing flip-flops. Lori actually spoke to me! Not only is she pretty, she's real nice too! Boy, if love at first sight really exists, I think I've found it! I wondered if I should turn around and look at her one more time. Would she be looking at me? I decided to look. When I turned around, Lori had been watching Sandy and me walk away. I tipped my hat to her and continued to walk on.

Walking the rest of the fair grounds, Sandy and I checked out all the rides. My three favorites were the Ferris wheel, Dodgem Cars and the wooden rollercoaster. I decided that if I had time at the end of the day, I would try one of them.

The stands around the Rodeo Circle were packed. Balloons, popcorn and hotdogs were being sold by some of the middle school boys. Wearing red and white pinstriped shirts, with a concession box strapped around their neck, they were shouting to the stands, "Hotdogs! Popcorn! Get your balloons here!"

Scanning the crowd, I searched for a glimpse of Lori; I really hoped she would make it. While searching, I saw Shannon with her best friend, Gail. Gail's sister, Rebecca, was a junior, and she was there too. As I watched them, I saw Rebecca waving to someone, motioning to someone to sit with them. Unbelievably, it was Lori! I realized that it made sense for Rebecca and Lori to know each other; they were both in the same grade, one year behind me.

Eventually, Lori joined the girls. Shannon was pointing my way. I think she was telling Lori that I was her brother. As I watched, Lori looked my way and our eyes met. Neither one of us quickly looked away, rather we both sat motionless for what seemed a very long moment. She was the first to look away and then continued talking to Shannon. My thoughts of Lori took over; *boy, she sure is pretty!*

Having her there began to make me a little bit nervous. I guess you could say I had a few butterflies in my stomach. "Okay, Sandy, Lori's here. We've gotta look our best. Show her you're the best barrel racer in the whole U, S of A! Now, let's ride! Yee Haw!"

Standing on the starting line, Sandy and I began the race with a quick burst of Sandy's muscle power. We were off. Holding close to the first barrel, he circled it with perfect form. Never depending on my reins, I guided Sandy with my body and legs, and he instinctively remained tight around the final two barrels. Sandy darted to the finish line where our official time was taken. It was an amazing record setting 13.2 seconds.

Applause and shouts of joy streamed from the stands. I have always appreciated the excitement of the crowd, but on this day I was searching for one particular member of the crowd. Was Lori applauding for me as well? Finally spotting her, I could tell she was happy for me. Looking at me, she stood up, raised her hands, clapped the air, and shouted something I couldn't make out. I took my hat off, and with a wink, I gave her a wave, and Sandy and I left the ring.

After each contestant finished the barrel race, the final scores were tallied and posted. The results confirmed that Sandy and I had won. Sandy, not I, deserved the credit for the win. He is the one who won that race; I was just along for the ride. Instinctively, Sandy has always known the course.

After finishing my final rodeo event, I decided to see if I could find Lori. The first place I decided to check was her father's recruitment booth. Standing inside the booth was an incredibly large, extremely fit man, wearing a military uniform.

"Hello, Mr. Dune, I presume," I queried as I reached out to shake his hand. "My name is William Casey, and I have come to see your daughter, Lori. Is she still here, or has she gone home?"

Returning my handshake, Mr. Dune spoke, "It's nice to meet you William. Lori has gone home for the evening. She has decided to get a jump start on her biography report, but I will be sure to let her know you stopped by."

Warmly I spoke, "Thank you, Mr. Dune. I would appreciate that."

Wow, I thought to myself, *you wouldn't ever catch me doing homework on a Saturday night!*

Tired and disappointed at not seeing Lori, I headed home myself.

Mom left a plate for me in the fridge. Stripping the foil off, I grabbed a fork and devoured my meal. I was much hungrier than I realized. After I finished my dinner, I jumped into the shower. As the warm water washed over my back, I became well aware of how sore my muscles felt. That night's shower lasted a bit longer than usual.

Falling into bed, I was completely exhausted. The events of that day gave me much to think about, especially meeting up with Lori. I wished that Dad were there so I could talk to him about her. I was never very interested in girls before; I wasn't sure how I should go about getting to know her better. I sure didn't know what to make of all those feelings I was starting to have. I wondered what Dad would tell me? What kind of advice would he have given me? As I lay there, I kept trying to imagine the words he would have used. He probably would have said something about being a gentleman and being myself, rather than conjuring up some personality I thought Lori might like better.

It was more painful than ever to realize that I wouldn't be able to share each new milestone with Dad. It's sometimes hard to explain, but when certain things occurred in my life, moments when I experienced something I never knew before, I found myself overwhelmed with a familiar sorrow. I would feel that devastating emotion I felt the day my dad died, the exact sadness I felt then. I don't think the realization of Dad's death ever got completely wrapped around my brain. It's as though my mind can't or won't accept his passing. My brain, somehow, preferred the denial mode. I really wished I could tell him about Lori.

Chapter 12
Holding on by a Thread

Our Sundays usually began with a big family breakfast followed by church. Father Ray Mendez is the new priest at St. Mary's, and my mom thinks he's wonderful. I agree; he's kind of cool for a priest. I think it's because he doesn't act "all spiritual," instead, he talks to me as though he was a good friend. Standing in judgment of others was something he didn't do either; he said that was something he left up to the Lord Almighty. "After all," he would often say, "Even Jesus didn't come to judge, but rather to save the lost. That's my job too, Will. I look after the lost."

Lately, he had been very worried about his friends and family still living in Cuba. The Premier of Cuba, President Fulgencio, was about to leave the country or be overthrown. It was reported that many did not like President Fulgencio's young wife, believing she craved power and control, and the Cuban people would not stand for it, especially the university students. But what truly worried Father Mendez was a man by the name of Fidel Castro. Hiding his whereabouts, he was vowing to save Cuba from such tyranny, but something within Father's spirit told him to be weary of this man.

Before many of the university students started terrorizing Cuba with riots and killings, it was a beautiful, thriving place. But as of late, things seemed to be going terribly wrong. I was able to tell all of this was weighing heavily on Father Mendez's mind.

I was amazed to learn that even as a young boy, living in Cuba, Father Mendez knew he wanted to become a priest. He often said to me,

"God had a plan and a purpose for my life, just as he does for you, Will, and for all of His children."

I couldn't help but question his philosophy, given that God allowed my Dad to die. How could that have been God's plan for Dad, for me, for any of us?…and what about Sarah? Was that God's plan as well? All I knew was that I had my own plans for Dad. And I would have loved to be able to share my life with Sarah, but those plans abruptly ended.

One of his Sunday morning homilies was about putting our faith in God, and when we have faith, we have hope. He said, "Hope is a joyful and confident expectation of God's earthly and eternal plan." He explained that without faith, we couldn't please God. If we lack faith in God, we lack real hope in our future and of what God can do in our lives. I concluded that there must have been many times when I hadn't pleased Him. Losing Sarah and Dad has placed my faith in a very fragile state, and what little hope I have left is holding on by a very thin thread.

Father Mendez always ended his sermon on an encouraging note. Most of the time, his closings explained that God wants each of us to come to Him just as we are, that God loves us in spite of our shortcomings. I was thankful for that! There have been far too many days when shortcomings could have been my middle name!

After church, I headed over to the Oktoberfest for its final day. Bull riding was the first event, and it started at twelve-thirty. My absolute favorite Rodeo event has always been the bull riding! Gregg tried to talk me into bowing out of this particular competition as well, but to no avail; I politely refused. I knew there was a chance I could get hurt. Lord knows, I had sustained plenty of injuries in the past; but, this was one time I really needed to ride the bull and Gregg knew it.

On more than one occasion, I remember hearing Gregg tell my dad he loved to see me ride the bull; that once I was mounted on its back, the bull and I became one. He said he'd never seen anyone with the coordination, balance and flexibility I had for such an event. An accolade like that, coming from a man of his distinction, was awe-inspiring and a little humbling.

The bull riding event had seen its first two contestants, one falling at the four second mark and the other holding strong until the end. Jimmy Pete held strong until the end, but his bull hadn't kicked once. He just spun Jimmy around in circles for the entire eight seconds. If I could get my bull to spin and kick, my chances of beating his score were very good.

Standing in the chute gate, I pulled the tail of my rope through a loop I had made, and then wrapped the rope securely around my fingers good and tight. I took a deep breath, made the sign of the cross, and gave the nod. The chute gate opened.

Holding on for eight seconds was going to be difficult; I had a "real live one" on my hands; Mad Jack was his name. Not only did Mad Jack like to keep spinning in one spot, he had one monster of a kick as well. Right from the get-go, he tried to throw me off his back by lunging forward, dipping his head to the ground, and kicking up his hind end. I had all I could do to hang on.

As I tried desperately to ride it out, I was able to keep my cool, and I tried to keep my body as flexible as possible. If I held out long enough, I believed I had a shot at first place. Half of my score depended on how much bucking and kicking the bull liked to do, and Mad Jack liked to do it a lot.

I was able to stay on for the full eight seconds. I swiftly unwrapped my hand, and then I jumped off as fast as I could and ran for the open gate. As I ran, two rodeo clowns distracted the bull away from me. Mad Jack was looking for me; you could be sure of that! I don't know whose job is more dangerous—the clown or the rider?

The last two events of the rodeo were the steer wrestling competition, and the tie-down roping. These events weren't scheduled to happen until later that day, so I decided to head out to the fair grounds in search of some pizza and a nice cold drink.

Bart had been waiting for me to finish; he joined me at the gate. "Good job, Will! You did great! I don't know how ya do it. You're sure crazy, if you ask me!"

"It's like free-falling, Bart. I feel completely alive when I'm on the back of a fast moving horse, or an ornery bull for that matter. I guess it's just something I was meant to do."

"Well, you couldn't find me closer than a hundred yards from Mad Jack; he's the meanest bull they've got! And when I say one hundred yards, I mean on the other side of the fence too!" Bart spoke with true certainty.

Bart was also in the mood for pizza, and Sergie's Pizza was his favorite. They served a pizza role that could be compared to no one! Thankfully, Bart said they had a booth set up and suggested we go there. That sure sounded great to me, so we headed in that direction.

As we made our way through the fair grounds, Bart and I saw Rebecca, Gail's sister. Bart asked if I would meet him at Sergie's; he wanted to go talk to her.

When I got to Sergie's, they didn't have any more pizza roles. So, I ordered two slices of pizza, loaded with everything, (except anchovies), and a Coke. A bench, next to the cotton-candy tent, was unoccupied; so, I decided to sit and wait for Bart. I had finished my first slice of pizza and was starting on my second when Bart showed up. Disappointed that they were out of pizza roles, he too ordered pizza slices and came to sit with me.

In between bites, we began a casual conversation. "How's Rebecca?" I asked.

With a strange expression on his face, Bart told me he had a date for next Friday night. I thought that was great, but I couldn't figure out why he wore such a peculiar expression. Something was up his sleeve, but I wasn't sure what.

Bart kept going on and on about the movie he was taking Rebecca to see. "Friday night's movie is, *North by Northwest*, starring Eva Marie Saint, James Mason and Leo G. Carroll. It's supposed to be a great suspense movie, some espionage thing. Alfred Hitchcock directs it, and you know what a master of suspense he is!"

I tried to act somewhat interested, "Yea, that's great Bart. Have fun."

How would you like to come with us?"

What was Bart thinking? "No thanks, Bart. Two's company; three's a crowd."

That thing up Bart's sleeve was about to come out. I could read it in his eyes. "Will, where did you get the number three? According to my calculations, the number is four."

What was he talking about? If he had gone and found me a blind date, I would be tempted to slug him (best friend or not). "What are you talking about, Bart!"

Hot under the collar, was an understatement! Bart needed to explain himself pretty darn quick, or he'd find himself in a heap of trouble. Cautiously, Bart began to share with me some very interesting news that he swore would make me happy.

"As you know, I asked Rebecca to go to the movies with me Friday night. She told me that it sounded like fun, but that she had other plans. She had already invited Lori Dune over for dinner and cards. Rebecca said that Lori only moved here a short time ago and hadn't made many friends yet. She wanted to make her feel welcome." As Bart rambled on, I still hadn't figured out what any of this had to do with me, but I had a scary feeling I was about to find out. "So, I had this great idea!" Bart spoke with cautious excitement. "Maybe Lori would like to go to the movies with us? And maybe, Will, you would like to go too?"

Shocked and stunned, I couldn't believe Bart would suggest such a thing. If I were going to go on a date, I would do the asking. I knew he was trying to be a friend, knowing that I liked Lori, but I didn't want our first date (if any date at all) to be done this way. "I'm sorry, Bart, but you can count me out," I told him.

Understandably, Bart was disappointed. This most likely meant his date with Rebecca was off as well, but thankfully, he handled it admirably. He said it was no problem. He understood, and he respected my position. Bart asked me if I would go with him to explain the situation to Rebecca. He wanted to see if she would go out with him another time.

Feeling this was the least I could do, I said I would.

We found Rebecca at the games. She was trying to shoot some little ducks at a game called Duck Hunting. Surprisingly, her aim appeared to be very good. As she and Bart were talking, I spotted Lori heading our way. My hair stood up on my arms, and my palms got all sweaty. That had never happened to me before, and I didn't like it. As Lori got closer I realized how bad I must smell. Bull Riding lends much to the sweat glands, if you know what I mean.

Rebecca hadn't told Lori about Bart's bright idea, so no harm had been done; I still felt rather awkward. Surprisingly, this time, Lori said hi to me first. "Hi, Will, I saw you at the bull riding today. You were really good. I don't know how you are able to stay on him for so long?"

The thoughts in my head began reeling! Talk about joy! I couldn't believe Lori came to watch me! "Thank you, Lori. It's something my dad once taught me. He was the best teacher a kid could ever have."

Lori looked at me with a rather strange, peculiar look. "You talk as if he's past tense."

I never expected one of my first conversations with Lori to be about my dad. "My dad died a few months ago."

With a sad look in her eyes, she said, "I'm sorry, Will. Unfortunately, I know all too well how it feels to lose one of your parents. My mom died two years ago in a car accident. It's still very difficult for me to accept. I don't think anyone ever gets completely over something like that."

Someone who had an inkling of how I felt! I couldn't believe it. I didn't know what to say. "I'm sorry you lost your mom, especially in that way. One of the things I've learned is not to take the people in my life for granted anymore; I appreciate my friends and family more than ever, now. Knowing my dad, I'm sure he would be glad to hear that coming from me!"

Lori told me later, that it was at that time she began to see a part of me she hadn't noticed before. She had observed that not many guys allowed their emotions to show, but was happy to see that I knew how to express my feelings in a wise and gentlemanly kind of way. Lori was impressed. "That's a wonderful attitude, Will. I agree with you."

I felt like I needed to make the atmosphere a bit lighter. I suggested the four of us check out the Ferris wheel and Old Woody (the wooden rollercoaster). Everyone thought that was a great idea.

Once we got to the ride, I asked Lori if she would like to share a cart with me. I was thrilled when she said yes. From that point on, the four of us had a great time. We chose to go on a few more rides, eat some sugar bread, and then play a few games. And believe it or not, I was able to win Lori a huge, stuffed panda bear at the famous ring toss. She loved it!

The last two rodeo events were about to start, so I told the 'guys' I needed to get going. They said they wanted to come and watch. Talk about nervous excitement! I was excited Lori would be there, but nervous that I might make some crazy mistake. The last thing I wanted to do was get hurt in front of her; or worse yet, make a fool of myself.

Thankfully, I did all right. I actually won the tie-down roping competition and came in second for the steer wrestling. I was grateful that I hadn't made any huge blunders, and actually placed with pretty good scores.

That night, as I lay in my bed, I found myself thinking about Lori. I really wanted to see if she would go out on a dinner date with me. Before I asked her, however, I felt there was something I needed to do first. I decided I would go do it the next day, first thing after school.

Chapter 13
May I, Major Dune?

As soon as school let out, I headed down Cayey Lane. My heart was beating fast and my breath came in gulps. I reached the building next to Leslie's Beauty Shop. Arriving at the door, I saw Lori's dad sitting at a desk examining some papers. He had an extremely grim look on his face, a look so grave one would think he was working on something that could change the course of world history.

"Hello, Mr. Dune. My name is William Casey. Do you remember me from the other day at the Oktoberfest?"

The major smiled and extended his hand. "Yes, I remember you, Will. How are you?"

As I shook his hand, I realized how nervous I was. Before today, I couldn't ever remember being afraid or nervous to talk to anyone. My first instinct was to run, but due to the extreme courage it took to get this far, I wasn't going to back down now. "I'm doing just fine, Mr. Dune. Thank you for asking. I have come here to ask you something."

Looking at me, with his left eyebrow lifted, his forehead wrinkled with obvious curiosity, and with a very somber demeanor, he told to me to go ahead and ask. Standing there, I was very aware of how fast my heart was pounding. A flashback suddenly came to me. I began to remember back to the last time my heart beat with such irregular force. I was giving my first oral presentation in our ninth grade English class. I passed out that day, in front of my entire class. *Oh, Lord, don't let me pass out today!*

I thought I should sit down. "May I have a seat, Mr. Dune?" Resting in a chair, I forced the words from my mouth; I asked for his permission to take Lori out on a date.

He looked at me now with both brows raised, and with that serious scowl that frightened me earlier. Mr. Dune looked me straight in the eye, and proceeded to ask me a question. He wanted to know why I wanted to take Lori out on a date.

I was not prepared for a question; in fact, I was rather prepared to hear a 'no.' At that moment, even though I was much more comfortable sitting than standing, I decided a man would stand. So I stood, and looked Mr. Dune right back in the eye, and I answered his question as honestly and as straightforward as I could. "Actually, Mr. Dune, Major, I find Lori to be the most interesting young lady I have ever met. She is bright, kind and refreshingly genuine. Lori has a sweet personality wrapped in a delightful sense of humor. You see, Mr. Dune, up until I met Lori, I had absolutely no interest in dating. My teenage years have been filled with horses and racing. I never wanted anything or anyone to take me away from that. But, for the first time ever, I have found a young lady that has caused me to pause in this life of mine and think about something other than horses and racing. I'll never give up horses and racing, but I believe I have found a girl I would love to share those things with. I like her a whole lot, Sir. And if she wants to, and if you will allow me to, I would be honored to take her out for a nice dinner and possibly even a movie."

Unbelievably, he granted his permission; he said, "Yes!" His consent, however, didn't come without some strict guidelines. Warning me, he explained that Lori was not only his daughter, but she was his pride and joy and the most important person in his life. He said he would do anything to protect her. With stern soberness, he mapped out his specifications. At all times, I was to act like a gentleman and treat her with dignity and respect. She was to be in by eleven o'clock and not one minute later. And finally, I was never to touch an adult beverage while responsible for her safety.

I agreed.

After leaving the Major's office, I gasped for a normal breathing pattern. I sat on a nearby bench and inhaled a large mouthful of air. As

I sat there, I realized that that was the first time since Dad died that I was truly happy and looking forward to the future. I felt hopeful and exhilarated. Life was good.

As torturous and distressing as it was approaching Mr. Dune, it was "a piece of cake" in comparison to actually asking Lori out. Once I got up the nerve to finally ask her, she said, "No." I remember the expression on her face as the words left her mouth. Looking as though she actually wanted to say, "Yes," she instead thought of every reason why she should say, "No." Lori had dreams and aspirations of her own. If I were to enter the picture, I might crowd out some of her ambitions. There just wasn't any room for me in Lori's world. She wanted to become a doctor one day, and that meant many hours of study, both here at school, and then later in college. Lori had no time for whimsical affections, and there was no way on God's green earth that she was going to allow herself to fall in love!

For quite some time, we continued on as friends. Lori occasionally came over to the farm to see Sandy. I was certain that something was happening between us. There was a kind of chemistry. She was starting to feel the same way I did; I was sure of it.

I will never forget the day I became certain of Lori's feelings toward me. We had gone to Chubb's Big Scoop for ice cream. My flavor choice was a vanilla-chocolate twist, and Lori ordered plain chocolate. Insisting that it be my treat, I paid the lady at the ice-cream window. Very few words were spoken as we ate our cones. Throughout this quiet time, we shared several glances. As I looked at Lori, I felt happy and totally complete. Our eyes met. Our gaze lasted for only a moment, and then we quickly looked away. For me, it was sheer torture. Each time our eyes met, the tension grew. I already knew that I had fallen in love with her, and I just hoped she felt the same.

Once we finished our cones, I suggested we go and get Sandy and take a ride down to the river. Surprisingly, she said, "Yes."

Once we got to the barn, I pulled Sandy by the reigns and led him out to the path, down toward the river. After I hopped on his back, I beckoned Lori to join me. Once on Sandy's back, she wrapped her arms around my waist and we rode, never speaking a word.

Sandy carried us to the river. We hopped off, and I let Sandy's reigns drop to the ground. The river was breathtakingly beautiful as autumn leaves clothed the banks of the water's edge. Brilliant colors of orange, yellow, red and variegated shades of green dressed the limbs of every tree.

As we sat mesmerized by the river's beauty, I turned to Lori and reached for her hand. She didn't pull back or resist, but rather, began to softly caress the palm of my hand. I looked into her eyes, which were the color of brilliant sapphire, and I began to openly share my feelings. The emotions I had for Lori were incredibly foreign to me. I had never felt this way about any girl before, and I needed to tell her that. I explained how my soul would leap and soar each time I was with her, and that the very core of my being longed to have her in my life as more than a friend. I was in love with her, and I wanted to know if she felt the same.

Lori didn't pull her hand away. She looked at me for what felt like an eternity. Thoughts whirled in my brain. Would she allow her reasoning to cloud her emotions? Did she love me, as I loved her? The anticipation of her reply was agonizing! I worried that I had destroyed our friendship, if, indeed, she didn't feel the same as I did.

A tear rolled down Lori's cheek as she revealed her love for me as well. She explained the determination to stay the course she had mapped out for herself, not wanting to allow herself to fall in love with me. It wasn't until that very moment that she gave into her feelings.

From that day forward, Lori and I became nearly inseparable. I vowed to support her completely in her endeavors to become a doctor, and she promised to stand by my side and encourage my passion for racing. As I continued on with my training, she continued to study. When Lori wasn't studying, she joined Gregg, Sandy and me at the track as we prepared for the championship race. Whether we were racing or in some way grooming Sandy for the big event, Lori tried to be there.

June came, and so did graduation. Graduation has always been a huge event in our town, our rite of passage as Mom says. Our class sizes are small enough that practically the entire town can fit in the school auditorium. This year, our class size was a whopping twenty-eight.

I was thrilled that this stage of schooling was over for me. I graduated with average grades, B' and C's, and I was very satisfied with my standing. I won't be surprised if Lori graduates as valedictorian with a cum laude status. She has certainly worked hard enough to be awarded such accolades, and I hope that next year she will be.

Once school finally let out for the summer, and graduation came and went, Sandy's training became very intense. I knew it was hard for Lori to have to share our time with such a rigorous schedule, but she never complained. I vowed to be as understanding once she got into medical school. The days of concentrated training and hard work made the summer months fly by.

Soon it was August, the month of the championship race.

Chapter 14
Expected Triumph

August finally came and so had the championship race. I woke up that morning with a strange combination of excitement and apprehension. All the hard work and preparation that Sandy and I had put into this event were soon to be put to the test. I laid there for a while, trying to take in all that was to come. I began to think of all the people in my life that had encouraged me along the way, Mom, Jonathan, Shannon and the boys, Lori, Gregg, Dad and most importantly, Sandy. I would be forever grateful to each of them. Without them, I don't think I would have been ready for today.

The championship race was going to be more important than I thought. Gregg told me that two gentlemen were going to be there scouting for experienced riders. They ran a professional rodeo and quarter-horse track in Montana called, The All-American Cowboy Rodeo and Track. Having them there could mean a huge opportunity for future employment.

Turning toward the clock, I realized my trusty, five a.m. buzzer would soon sound. I closed my eyes, took a deep breath and climbed out of my bed. After turning off the alarm clock, I headed downstairs for my routine mug of milk and one of mom's delicious doughnuts. As I left the house, I breathed in the fresh, summer air. The weather report promised sunny skies and mild temperatures, a great day for a race.

Arriving at the barn, I greeted Sandy with a hug and tender strokes along his mane. "Are you ready for the day ahead, Sandy?"

With a neigh and a nod, he seemed to be telling me, "Yes, positively, yes!"

Grabbing his reigns, we made our way out to the field and rested on the ground until the sun made its final ascension. The colors of the sun were radiant shades of orange and yellow. Every time that sun takes its rise, I am reminded of Dad and how many mornings were shared by just the three of us. I really missed him. If I could have had him back for just one day, I would surely have picked that morning. Not only could I have used his advice and encouragement, but I really wanted to make him proud. I knew if Sandy and I could run the championship race with Dad cheering us on, it would be the perfect day! He could not be there in body, but I felt as if he were there in spirit that morning. I felt his presence like I had never felt it before.

Before Sandy and I headed back to the barn, I wanted to tell him a couple of things. "Sandy, today is our day. I want you to go out there and enjoy yourself like you've never done before. We are a team, you and I, and I'm so proud to have you in my life. When I sit on your back, and place my feet in those stirrups, and we race with the wind, I figure I'm one of the luckiest guys on this planet."

Sandy brushed his soft face against mine, and I knew he understood every word I said.

The smell of fried eggs and bacon were being carried in the breeze from the house. I took Sandy back to the barn and ran to the house for a hardy breakfast. Sure enough, Mom had been in our kitchen cooking a breakfast fit for a king. Preparing a hearty breakfast was one way Mom chose to show her support and encouragement. She said it was a breakfast fit for a champion. I chuckled, but Mom just stood there looking at me with all seriousness. She finally turned around and continued flipping her bacon as if to say, "It's decided."

The race was scheduled to begin promptly at ten, so I spent the little bit of time I had at home, showering, getting dressed, and finally getting Sandy ready. We headed for the track at eight-thirty. As we drove through the track gates, I could see that people had already arrived to pick their favorite seats. My family, Bart and Lori didn't need to worry about seating; I had arranged for all of them to sit in the first row.

Sandy and I had been at our stall for a few minutes when Lori and

Bart showed up to give me a pep talk. Bart stretched out his hand and began to offer his support. "Will, today belongs to you and Sandy. Take it!"

While shaking Bart's hand, I thanked him for all he had done for me; I told him that no one could ask for a better friend. Bart hugged Sandy and gave him a couple of reassuring pats on the head.

Lori reached out to take my hand, and then, on the tips of her toes, she embraced me with a hug. As we hugged, she spoke sweetly into my ear. "I love you, William Casey. You have worked so hard. Go win that race. You deserve it, both you and Sandy." And then Lori kissed my cheek. Before she could walk away, I reached up and gently cupped one side of her face, and I told her how much her love and support meant to me and that I loved her too. Then I pulled her close to me, and I softly kissed her. We then stood there in silence for a moment looking at each other. Lori reached up and touched my cheek with her hand and then walked away to encourage Sandy. She stroked the sides of his face and began talking with him. When their conversation had finished, she gave him a kiss on the cheek as well. Watching the woman I loved demonstrate such affection towards Sandy, nearly brought tears to my eyes. I was on top of the world, and I was so thankful.

Time had now come for me to head out to the track; so, Lori and Bart quickly headed for their seats.

Before Sandy and I made it to our gate, we took our customary side step. I took off my hat and waved to the crowd. A small section of the crowd erupted with loud shouting and clapping. Sandy seemed anxious as he tried to back away from the starting gate. I tried to soothe him, "Okay, Sandy! C'mon now boy; it's all right. This is our day. Stay calm, San. This one's for Dad." It was odd that Sandy would try to back out of the gate like that. I had a difficult time convincing him to get into place. I figured that the size of the crowd and all the noise shook Sandy up a bit. Finally, I was able to reassure and calm Sandy, allowing him to focus and prepare for the bell.

Once inside our gate, we waited for the bell to sound. As we sat there, I patted Sandy on the head and spoke to him, "Sandy, I love you, and you have been the greatest friend a guy could ever hope to have.

Whether we win or lose, we'll do it together. God speed, my friend!" I then whispered a short prayer of thanks, made the sign of the cross, and with the jitters and a rush of excitement, I got ready for a long awaited race. The bell sounded.

As the bell rang out, the horses darted out of their gates. Sandy was the first one out. His hooves pounded over the ground. Dirt and muck were scattered over the track in every direction. Sandy was a magnificent sight. Every sinew and every muscle was stretched to capacity as his long legs took determined strides to the inside rail.

With a quick glance behind, I could see our amazing lead. Just as I started to measure the rest of the stretch in front of me, I felt a jerk from Sandy. My world began to collide with his and terror rang through my soul and then all went black.

In the flash of a moment, as the spectators looked on, a terrible accident began to unfold before the horror-stricken crowd. Sandy dropped out of sight as he abruptly rolled forward with Will never leaving the saddle. It looked as though Sandy had stepped in a hole. He fell to the ground trapping Will beneath him. This was not the first time Sandy's speed advanced him to the lead; but this time, being in front led to peril, not triumph. The other horses were unable to avoid the downed rider and his horse, and soon each of them began to trample Will and Sandy beneath their hooves.

In the stands, a still hush replaced the previous clamor. In the deafening silence, prayers reached forth to the heavens as fear and anguish began to overshadow the earlier, lighthearted merriment.

William lay lifeless on the ground. The fear on Jonathan's face told a horrifying story. Panic permeated the air. Sandy was writhing in pain. He was a 1200-pound quarter horse, Will's best friend, and he lay atop him…

Gregg Pace gave Sandy something to help calm him down. Now, horse and rider both lay lifeless, and the sight was painfully eerie. An expected triumph had turned to shock and disbelief.

Chapter 15
The Dreaded Scene

Lori ran out of the stands as quickly as she could, screaming. "Will! Will! Please, get up. Will, Get up!" *Please, Lord God, make him get up! Lord, please, please, oh Lord God!*

Pushing her way through the crowd, Lori desperately tried to make her way to the track. The mass of people in her way seemed to be growing with her every step. Finally, she made it to the entrance and screamed for Gregg Pace to let her in. "Gregg, I need to see Will; please let me in! Gregg, Gregg! Let me in!"

It was no use. Gregg couldn't hear Lori over the din of the onlookers' cries and the added blast of a siren coming from beyond the gates. There was no hope of her cry being heard.

Officer Hopkins found Will's mother, Claire, and escorted her directly to the scene. Once she made it to Will's side, she gasped at what she saw. His body was lifeless, as blood streamed from his scull, soaking the ground underneath him. Will's head had been split from one ear clear around to the other. The medics carefully wrapped his head, applying pressure as best they could, until the ambulance arrived. The extent of Will's injuries weren't known for sure, but it was painfully obvious, given his contorted body, he had many, many broken bones.

Claire's cries were frantic. "Oh, Will, my baby, please don't die, Will." Claire stroked Will's face as she pleaded with God to save her son. "Dear God, don't let Will die; save my boy. I don't want to lose him, Lord. Please save him Lord, please, please…" Claire's sobs were heartbreaking for all who were there. It didn't seem to anyone present that Will could possibly survive such a dreadful accident.

Finally able to enter the inside track, the ambulance made its way toward Will. Jumping out of the ambulance, the medical personnel asked everyone to clear away. Eventually, Will was lifted from the ground up into the ambulance. One of the men caring for Will asked Claire if she would like to ride in the ambulance with him. Jonathan told her to go with Will, and he would meet them both at the hospital.

Before boarding, Claire asked Gregg if Sandy was going to be all right. Gregg just looked up at Claire with tear filled eyes; he closed them and shook his head no.

"We will miss you Sandy; you were an amazing friend, and we will never forget you," said Claire as she quickly boarded the ambulance. The doors shut behind her as fear and silence permeated the air. It seemed such a cold 'goodbye', leaving Sandy that way, but Claire could only think of one person right now, and that was clearly her son.

As Will was whisked away, his fate was still unknown. A horse trailer was brought to retrieve Sandy. As he was hoisted up, Sandy's head drooped to the side as if his neck were broken. His body was limp and motionless. He was hurt badly, and it was obvious to all that his life was hanging in the balance.

Bart finally caught up with Lori. He told her to come with him, and he would get her to the hospital. She only had one question, "How fast can you get us there?"

Chapter 16
The Long Wait

The Kateyville Hospital had been informed, and made special preparations for Will's arrival. An injury of this magnitude required the hospital's top surgeon, Doctor Brad Halbig. Dr. Halbig was head surgeon of the critical care unit at Kateyville Hospital. If anyone could save Will's life, this was the man most qualified to do it.

Dr. Halbig listened to the incoming message put out by the ambulance attendant bringing Will in. "The patient is William Casey."

Dr. Halbig knew right away who he was. *Oh Lord, no. Not William. Oh Claire!*

The first responder continued, "Patient is unconscious, severe head trauma, fractured skull; the patient has lost a great deal of blood. Simple fracture to jaw, compound fracture both collar bones, commensurate fracture to several ribs, open break to left femur, open abrasions left foot and left ankle, simple fracture right ankle. Internal injuries are unknown at this time."

Kateyville was a small, close-knit town, and most of the hospital personnel knew Will and his family. When word got out that it was Will being brought in, the staff was shocked and incredulous that another tragedy had befallen the Casey family. With steadfast resolve, they made ready to do all they could to save this young man's life.

When the ambulance arrived, Will was rushed to the critical care unit immediately. Dr. Halbig made preparations for the challenging surgery ahead; he only hoped Will was strong enough for the ordeal that lay before him. Did Will have the resolve to fight? He desperately hoped so.

Bart and Lori arrived shortly after the ambulance. They ran as fast as they could toward the emergency room. Desperate for answers, Lori pleaded with a nurse she spotted in the hall. "Where is William Casey? Did they bring him here? I need to know; is Will all right? Please help me; I need to see him!"

The nurse had a difficult time calming Lori down. Bart quickly stepped in. His heart broke for Lori, because he knew how much she loved Will. He understood all too well how frightened she was, but her hysteria clearly wasn't helping the situation. Bart urged Lori not to worry; he said he would find out all that he could. He gently urged her to have a seat and assured her he would return as quickly a he could.

As Bart approached the nurse's station, he composed himself as best he could. He implored the nurse behind the desk to tell him where they had taken William Casey, the young man who had been brought in by the ambulance from the Kateyville Track.

With a calm voice, the nurse told all she knew. She explained that Will had just been brought in and was taken up to the operating room for immediate surgery. "I realize how upset and frightened you must be; I wish I could tell you more. The best thing you can do…well, I'm sure his family is here by now. Go down the hall, and take the corridor to the right. Take it all the way to the end, and you will find a waiting room on your left. Will's family should be in there."

Bart was most thankful, "Thank you so much. We really appreciate your help." Lori and Bart quickly headed toward the waiting room.

Walking into the waiting area, Bart and Lori saw Claire, Jonathan and Shannon. Claire stood up and walked slowly toward Bart. She gave him a hug. "Thank you for coming, Bart. I know Will would want you here." Claire then hugged Lori and told her the same. With tears in her eyes, she told them how bad it was. "We need to pray. God is our only hope now."

Lori couldn't believe what she was hearing. How could this happen? Just this morning they were talking about what they were going to do after the race. Will said he wanted to do something fun to celebrate, something that included Sandy. Lori's thoughts turned to Sandy. *What about him? Was Sandy all right?*

Lori walked up to Jonathan and gave him a hug. "Is Susan with Lenny and Christopher?"

Jonathan's voice was shaky, but he was determined to stay strong for the family. "Yes, Susan took the boys home right from the track. They're pretty confused right now, but Susan has been trying to reassure them that Will's going to be all right. In fact, we're all trying to reassure ourselves of that."

Lori had to ask about Sandy. She needed to know that he was all right.

Jonathan's response was heartbreaking. "It doesn't look like Sandy made it, Lori. The fall broke his neck." With his eyes full of water, Jonathon tried his best to keep the tears from overflowing. But as one determined tear fell down his cheek, Jonathan painfully blurted out, "I just don't know how I'm going to tell Will, Lori. How am I going to do that? I just don't know! But as hard as that's going to be, I only hope God gives me that chance. I hope I see Will alive and well so that I can tell him."

Telling Will, well, that was a path nobody wanted to take. There wasn't one person in that room wanting to break Will's heart like that, but learning of Sandy surely would. When his dad died, Will was completely crushed, but Sandy was there, his best friend, to help heal Will's wounded heart. At the time of his rebellion, his parents credited this gentle creature with Will's rescue. Having Sandy to love and care for, Will was less inclined to yield to his seemingly wild and reckless nature.

It was Sandy who was able to catch Will's fall, to save him from certain destruction, to give him a purpose and a reason to do what was right and good. If Sandy were to indeed die, many feared Will's hope might surely die with him.

Chapter 17
Remembering Back

Dr. Brad Halbig had been a close friend of Claire's ever since they were little kids. Claire's family spent a great deal of time with his family while they were growing up. Their houses were directly across the street from each other. She never knew it, but Brad had been deeply in love with her ever since they were kids playing on Claire's front porch. Never having the nerve to tell her how he felt, he soon found out that any attempt was already too late. It was too late because Claire met Harry. It was ruefully plain to see, as Brad watched Claire with Harry, she was utterly taken with him. The way she looked at Harry, well, she never looked at him that way, and deep in Brad's heart, he knew she never would. Seeing the two of them so completely in love with each other, eventually prompted Brad to resign himself to the fact that he was out of the picture forever. He consoled himself with the knowledge that Claire was happy. Harry was a good man. Brad knew that Harry would take good care of Claire and would do all that he could to make her happy. Brad wanted that for Claire, even if it meant that his love for her would never be returned. Still, he very much valued Claire's friendship and didn't want to lose that. He vowed to himself he would never pursue her romantically, and he honored that pledge.

One of Dr. Halbigs's nurses came into the waiting room to speak with the family. Claire and Lori were the first to rise from their seats. "Hello, Mrs. Casey. My name is Robin, and I am one of the nurses working with Dr. Halbig. He wanted me to come out and speak with you to let you know what's happening with Will." Claire was so

99

thankful that it was Brad operating on Will. He had a sterling reputation as a surgeon and was one of Harry's and her dearest friends.

Claire urged Robin to continue.

"Dr. Halbig wanted you to know that he is doing everything he possibly can to help Will. He also wanted you to know that it's a positive sign Will has survived up until now. He has a very strong heart, and that is most likely why he was able to endure such physical trauma. As soon as he is able, Dr. Halbig will be out to speak with you personally."

After Robin's visit, everyone felt a sense of relief upon hearing a somewhat positive report. However, without knowing Will's final outcome, there was still an air of apprehension and anxiety in the room. It would be five more hours before they could finally speak with Dr. Halbig.

Shannon sat next to her mother and just held her close. "He's going to make it, Mom. I know he is; Will's a fighter, and he always has been. He won't give up now."

Claire desperately hoped Shannon was right. After hugging Shannon and giving her a kiss on the forehead, she got up and decided to walk the hallway for a bit. When she left the room, Bart took a seat next to Shannon. With eyes full of tears, he began to talk to her, "You're right, you know. Will is going to make it. He's the best friend I've got, and I'm not losing him today. You have my word on that."

Shannon and Bart hugged for a brief moment. Before Bart got up to pace the room again, Shannon told him she believed there was strength in numbers. So many people were pulling for Will, how could he not get better? Smiling at each other, they were comforted to learn how like minded they were concerning their belief in Will's recovery. They both wanted to believe Will was going to make it, because as far as they were concerned, anything else was unacceptable.

Eight hours had passed since Will first arrived at the hospital. Tired eyes instantly opened wide as Dr. Halbig entered the room. He extended his hands to Claire as she reached for his. He began to explain Will's condition. "Will is in a coma. He has suffered extreme head trauma. It's still too early to know if there will be any negative or lasting effects from the head injury. It is, of course, our hope that he won't. Will has also suffered a large number of broken bones. He has a broken collar-bone, six cracked ribs, a fractured knee cap, a broken jaw, as well as a very serious break of the left femur. We will do all that we can for him, Claire. You have my word."

Claire was eager to see Will. "When can I see him?"

Dr. Halbig spoke cautiously to Claire, "You may go in now, but only you. You may only stay for a very short time. Then, Claire, I think you should go home and get some sleep. Jonathan, make sure your mom gets home; will you, please?"

Jonathan assured Dr. Halbig that he would do just that, and he thanked him for all he was doing. "We love that boy in there, and we all want to see him walk out of here," said Jonathan.

"You have my word that we will continue to do all we can. It wouldn't hurt to send up a few prayers as well, Jonathan," said Dr. Halbig.

Brad led Claire down to Will's room. As Clair walked in, she began to quietly sob. Will's face was so badly bruised that she could hardly tell it was him. Gently, Claire touched his cheek. As she looked at him, memories of the past flooded her mind.

He was her third child. She remembered ever so clearly the day she delivered him. Not only had her pregnancy been difficult, with the premature labor that forced her into bed rest the last three months of her pregnancy, but so had the hours in the hospital just before his birth. Will never 'turned' as the doctors hoped he would. Delivering him breach was out of the question, so it was determined Claire would need surgery to remove Will. Claire prayed that her baby would be born healthy and strong. She feared that her difficult pregnancy might cause possible health problems for her child.

Later, when Claire awoke from her anesthesia, a jolt of panic penetrated her consciousness. "Harry, Harry, where are you! What happened to my baby? Harry!"

Immediately, Harry was at her side. "Claire, it's okay. We have a baby boy. Our little boy is going to be just fine. I'll go get the nurse; I'll have her bring him in right away."

Claire quickly spoke, "Wait, Harry. Hold me, please. Just hold me. I was so scared. I couldn't bear the thought of…"

Harry interrupted Claire in mid sentence, "Honey, we didn't lose him. He's here, and he's healthy. We're all going to be okay. Let me go get him for you. I'll be right back." Harry reached down and kissed Claire lightly on the lips.

Harry understood Claire's fear, due to the fact that her family history spoke volumes. Claire's mother lost two children, one stillborn and the other dying three months after birth. Both of Claire's sisters gave birth to stillborn children, and one of them suffered a miscarriage. No one knew why these things happened, and until Claire could be given a reason, each pregnancy she endured became her 'cross to bear'.

"I love you, darling. I love you." After lovingly patting her hand, Harry slowly left Claire's bedside and walked out of the room to find the nurse. When he returned, Harry had the baby in his arms. With tears welling up in his eyes, Harry handed the beautiful bundle to Claire.

After he gently placed the child in her arms, tears began to softly fall down her cheeks; she kissed the baby's face over and over again. "Oh, Harry, he's so beautiful. He looks just like you, Harry. What should we name him?"

Harry hadn't thought of a name for the baby. Growing up without a father, the only strong male role model in his life was his grandfather, William.

William owned several horses at Kateyville Stables. Harry hung out around the stables quite often, and his interest in horses didn't go unnoticed by William. William took Harry under his wing, and treated him as though he was his own son. He gave Harry a job cleaning the stables, and in return for his labor, he was given the opportunity to ride many of the horses there. It wasn't long before Harry took a strong liking to a beautiful, kind-tempered quarter horse named Jackson.

Several years after Harry had lived with his grandparents, Harry learned that William was married to someone else before his grandmother. He and his first wife had a son named Jimmy. At the age of four, Jimmy died from a severe asthma attack. Soon after, William's wife moved out and went to live with her parents back in Vermont. She never returned. The boy's death just put too much strain on their marriage and eventually ended it. Harry's grandmother said that difficult times either brought people together, stronger than ever, or it separated people beyond repair. She said it depended on what they were made of and what they had to "draw on" between them. So, as it turned out, Harry became like a real son to his grandfather, and William became the father Harry desperately wanted.

William died when he was ninety-two, and he died peacefully in his sleep. Harry missed him a great deal, but more than anything, he was thankful to have had him in his life.

Claire had an idea for a name, "How about William? I think that would be a fine name. What about you, Harry?"

Wrinkles began to form in the corners of Harry's eyes, as a large smile began to emerge across his face. "I would love that to be his name, William Casey."

Claire responded, "William Harry Casey."

Looking back, it was hard for Claire to believe that today Will could be in such peril, fighting for his life. All she could do now was pray; so looking down at Will, Claire dropped her head and began to plead with God for her son's life.

Chapter 18
Claire's Prayer

As Claire fixed her eyes on Will, a hopeless feeling came over her. She realized the only solace for her would be prayer, a prayer pleading for Will's healing and recovery. Dropping to her knees, Claire placed her elbows on the side of Will's bed, cupped her hands together, bowed her head, and began to cry. She quietly prayed, *"Dear Father God, healing is in Your hands—Yours alone. Your word says, 'by your stripes we are healed', and I take you at Your word today, by placing my son, Will, at Your feet. I ask you to have mercy on him, and make him well again. It's for Your mercy, I pray. Amen."*

As Claire's prayer ended, Dr. Halbig entered the room. As he looked at her, his heart grew heavy. He worried so much about her, realizing she had already been through so much this past year. Losing Harry was a devastating blow to her, but knowing she had children to care for, gave her the strength she needed to go on. What would happen to her now? Brad wanted to take her in his arms, comfort her, and make everything all right again. But he knew he couldn't, so instead, he directed all his energy and thoughts towards making Will well again.

Dr. Halbig reasoned with Claire, trying his best to convince her it was time she went home and got some rest. "There is nothing more you can do for Will today," he insisted. "I promise someone will be with him at all times. He will get around the clock care. Your family needs you, and you need them. Please go home, Claire."

Claire tried to make a case for staying. "How can I leave him? I'm so scared, Brad. I'm just so afraid to leave him."

As Claire began to cry, Brad knew as a friend, he must comfort her. So, he reached for Claire and hugged her gently, simply allowing her tears to flow. Brad had all he could do not to cry himself.

Pulling herself together as best she could, Claire joined the others in the waiting room. Jonathan put his arm around Claire and slowly led her out of the building.

Susan met them at the door as soon as they arrived back at the house. "Claire, the boys are sleeping peacefully in their beds. I have kept a dinner warm for you. I'll put it on the table for…"

Claire interrupted Susan, "Oh, thank you darling, but I can't eat. I think I will just get ready for bed. The boys will be up and around early as usual, and I'll need to be well rested for our day ahead. But, thank you Susan for all you've done. You're a blessing, and I appreciate you very much."

Susan saw the fatigue and worry on her mother-in-law's face, and only wished she could do more to help. Jonathan was also on her mind. Being strong, and not letting on how he truly felt, was what he did best. Maybe this evening he would allow himself to let his guard down and let her console him. She wondered if telling Jonathan about her visit with the doctor today would be a good idea. After a great deal of thought, Susan decided she would wait for a better time to share her news.

Eventually, Claire was ready for bed, and Jonathan kissed her good night. "Mom, call me, no matter what time it is, and I will be here for you. Do you hear me, Mom? Any time."

With a mother's resolve, Claire tried to comfort Jonathan, "John, please honey, I'll be fine. You need to get some sleep yourself. Just call me in the morning so we can figure out a schedule. I want someone to be with Will at all times."

Claire was awakened by the telephone. She couldn't believe she had slept so late. It was already eight o'clock. Why hadn't the boys awakened her yet? After putting slippers on her feet, Claire headed for the kitchen. Much to her surprise, Lenny and Christopher had breakfast all ready for her at the breakfast nook. They had prepared whole-wheat toast, peanut butter, corn flakes, orange juice and the strongest cup of coffee she'd ever tasted. How could she not drink it? The boys put so much effort into her breakfast. Taking them in her arms she said, "You boys are the best. Thank you, so much!"

Christopher spoke first, "We know Will is hurt real bad, and we knew how upset you are. We just wanted to do something nice for you, to try to make you feel better."

Lenny chimed in, "Yeah, and we wanted to let you sleep in. Susan said you were real tired, and we should try to be quiet when we got up this morning. We didn't wanna wake you up."

Their conversation was interrupted by a knock on the door. It was Barb Davis, Claire's closest friend. In her hands was a baked lasagna, garlic bread, apple pie and vanilla ice cream for the boys. "I didn't want you to have to worry about making any meals. A group of us women got together, and, let's just say, you shouldn't have to worry about cooking for your family for quite a while. I'm so sorry Claire; if there is anything I or any of the rest of us can do…"

Claire politely broke in, "You have done enough; all I need now is your prayers. We can't lose him, Barb. We just can't." Again, Claire's eyes began to fill up with tears.

Barb's heart ached for her; so, placing the meal down, Barb held her dear friend in her arms.

Claire and Barb have been there for each other during life's hardest moments, and today was no different. Barb lost her husband a year prior to Harry's death. Richard Davis had suffered through a long bout with cancer that eventually got the best of him. Without Claire, Barb doesn't know how she could have coped.

Before Barb left, she assured Claire that Will would be in her prayers, and that some of the parishioners at church were getting together with Father Mendez to start a prayer vigil. "Will's going to make it, Claire. In my heart, I just know it." Barb left, but said she would soon return to pick up Christopher and Lenny. She didn't want Claire worrying about the boys.

Shannon was still sleeping. She had stayed at the hospital until very late talking with Lori and Bart. They couldn't bear to leave. If they weren't in the waiting room, they were in the hospital cafeteria awaiting any kind of news. At one point Lori looked at the clock. Seeing that it read three-thirty she knew her father would have wanted her home and thought she had better get going. Bart offered to give Lori and Shannon a ride. After he dropped the girls off, he headed back to the hospital to spend the night at Will's bedside. Frightened at the possibility of losing his best friend, there wasn't another place on the face of the earth where he wanted to be.

Chapter 19
Sandy's Last Hour

The trailer that took Sandy from the track went through the far gate out onto Cayey Lane. Gregg Pace followed close behind, as the trailer made its way to Dr. Debra Brown, Kateyville's veterinarian. A phone call had already been made, informing Debra of Sandy's condition. She had been Sandy's vet for several years, and she knew him well. Hearing of his condition worried and saddened her. It had been clear by the report that Sandy would probably not make it.

As Gregg drove Sandy to the vet's place, his hands began to grip the steering wheel with such force his knuckles turned white. Slowly, his bottom lip began to quiver as the initial shock of all that had happened began to wear off. Raw emotion took hold and flooded his mind. Sandy wouldn't survive the accident, and the boy he thought of like a son, might not make it either. His thoughts rambled, *"How could things have gone so wrong? What happened out there? How could we have missed it? Something was on that track that wasn't supposed to be there. What in God's name went wrong?"* A tear made its slow decent down Gregg's cheek.

Sandy's trailer began to turn, slowly making its way toward the Veterinarian Hospital. Dr. Brown's hospital was a one-hundred-year-old barn, refurbished to perfectly fit her needs and the needs of the animals she cared for. Debra waved the trailer in.

Horses like Sandy didn't come along very often, especially one as strong, as fast, and one with such a gallant heart. In the past, when treating Sandy, Debra would often say, "Sandy is such a special creature; he's also kind of an enigma. He has such a gentle soul, soft, quiet and affectionate, while yet possessing a strong, determined and fearless kind of competitiveness." In her eyes, it was easy to see that Sandy was much more than just a horse; he was a friend, Will's loyal and trusted friend.

Backing up to the barn, Gregg saw Debra. After directing the trailer toward the large barn doors, she opened them, revealing a large crane. Eventually the crane would be attached to Sandy's twinging body, and then he would be hoisted up and placed on a table for whatever procedure came next.

Opening the door of his truck, Gregg slowly placed both feet onto the ground. As he made his way toward Sandy and Debra, he hoped that somehow he had been wrong—that Sandy wasn't as bad off as he thought, and that maybe he would make it. But, in his mind, he knew differently.

Reaching out his hand, Gregg greeted Dr. Brown. "Thanks for meeting us here so fast. Sandy's in bad shape."

"He's such a grand creature, and I know how much he's loved by Will…and all of you. I want to do all I can. Now, let's go take a look at him. You said he's been hurt real bad…"

"Yea, Doc, he's real bad off."

Dr. Brown jumped up to the bed of Sandy's trailer. The black flies had already started to pester him. Sandy did his best to wink them away; lifting his neck was no longer possible. Debra waved the flies away in a gesture of concern, knowing this once noble creature could no longer fend for himself.

Debra's thoughts raced back to memories of this horse lying before her. She remembered a kind-hearted stallion, once grand, strong and beautiful. Today, Sandy did not exhibit those qualities. He was badly bruised. He had been trampled by the other horses and was now quivering and writhing with pain. The left side of his face had been crushed, both hind legs appeared broken, and there were several deep lacerations on his body. But the worst injury Sandy sustained was that of a broken neck.

As Dr. Brown examined Sandy's neck and spinal area, she showed

Gregg the location of the break. It was an irreversible injury. Tears began to fill Dr. Brown's eyes. Sandy wasn't going to make it, and now they both knew it for sure.

She knew putting Sandy to sleep was not going to be easy, but she didn't want Sandy to suffer any longer. The injuries he had received were causing him a great deal of agony.

Sandy's eyes were open, and he was looking around. Horses are generally quite smart, but Sandy was especially so; and he knew something was terribly wrong. Desperate to pick up his head, Sandy's eyes scanned the area around him as best he could, most likely searching for Will.

Gregg kneeled down in front of Sandy. "Sandy! Hey, boy! It's me, Gregg. It's okay, buddy. The Doc's gonna make the pain stop. I'll be right here. I'm not going anywhere. Will can't be here, buddy, but you know he would if he could. He loves you more than anything in this world."

Tears were now streaming down Gregg's cheeks; he stroked Sandy's face and nose. Mumbling words of sorrow and regret, Gregg tried to comfort Sandy. Soon he looked up at Debra, but words defied him. He knew if he spoke, he would lose control, and the sobs within would burst out. Gregg turned back and continued petting Sandy.

Debra looked at Gregg, and while placing her hand on his shoulder, she forced out the words no one wanted to hear. "I need to put him to sleep." Debra's eyes closed, fighting back the tears, "I'm going to go get what I need, and I'll be right back."

Gregg never looked up, and didn't speak a word; he just nodded. He knew what had to be done.

After placing her hand on Sandy's head, and stroking his back, Debra stepped away and disappeared behind the barn doors.

Stroking him gently, Gregg realized he had no choice but to allow his tears to flow. Knowing what lay ahead, there was just no stopping them. In a matter of moments Sandy's life here on earth would be over and his fate sealed.

Gregg whispered in his ear and began to tell him how much he cared for him. "Sandy, I've been around many, many horses in my life. Some were magnificent creatures that could run like lightening, some had a knack for the rodeo, and some just stood strong and proud in a pasture of their own. But you, my friend, you stand above all of them. Do you know why you stand above all the rest? Is it your speed? No. Is it your agility? No. Your accuracy? No. It's because you have heart and soul. It was easy to see that you wanted Will to be proud of you, and he is. Without you, Will's life would have been in shambles. You saved him. You became the miracle that healed his broken, guilt-ridden heart. I know you're worried about him, but I believe he's going to be all right. I don't want you to worry. A part of you will always be with Will, and you'll keep helping him. I just know it."

For a moment Gregg's thoughts shifted to Will and his welfare. If Will survived the accident, Gregg knew his broken bones could heal, but what about his broken heart? He knew full well that Will's fate was now dangling on the last knot in his rope, and he wondered how long he could hang on. Looking down at Sandy, he feared thinking about the possible answers to his questions.

Gregg continued his conversation with Sandy. "When you get up there, to Heaven, could you talk to the big guy? You need to be our messenger, and let God know Will's going to need him. And when you see Sarah and Harry, ask them to pray for Will; although, I bet they already are. He's going to need a lot of prayers. He's really gonna need 'em."

Just as Gregg finished his talk with Sandy, Debra arrived. It was about to be finished, and an overwhelming sadness, the kind a person gets when someone they love is passing away, that phobic feeling of finality, well, that feeling filled Gregg and crushed him to his inner core.

Debra looked at Gregg, "Are you ready, Gregg? I'll wait until you're ready, and you've said your goodbyes."

Gregg looked down at Sandy, stroked his face, and bent down to kiss him on the cheek. Gregg whispered in his ear, "I love you, Sandy. Will loves you, Sandy. We're all going to miss you, buddy. Oh God, we're really gonna miss you!"

Looking at Debra, Gregg nodded. Gently, Debra knelt down and gave Sandy his injection. Within sheer moments, Sandy was gone. Debra left Gregg alone with the animal, and Gregg just sobbed, holding Sandy in his arms.

Chapter 20
Will's Dream

Strangely, I find myself sitting by the side of a river. Before me, I see a beautiful place on the other side. Over there the sun is shining brightly; the flowers are blooming with brilliant shades of pink, red, blue, violet and yellow. They appear to be perfect, flawless in every detail. The grass is a luminous, yet a soothing shade of green, also perfect, down to each symmetrical blade. I am able to see many people who appear to be having a fabulous time. They are smiling and waving at me. I can hear beautiful singing. Everyone looks so happy. Dancing in the sky overhead, I can see all kinds of radiantly colored butterflies and birds. Oh, the sun seems to not only be providing heat and beams of light but also a kind of supernatural joy.

Suddenly, I see seven lily pads appear before me. They seem to be beckoning me to step on them and cross over to the other side, to this beautiful place. I do feel very eager to go there. I think I'll hop on each pad and see how far I can go. Soon, there was only one more lily pad to go, and I knew if I stepped on it, I could reach the other side. I looked back to see how far I had come. On the riverbank behind me, I saw my mother, my brothers and my sister. They looked very sad, and they were crying. The lily pads began to move apart. I knew they would soon be too difficult to reach.

Instinctively, I knew I had to make a decision. Did I want to go back and be with my family and friends, or did I want to go to that beautiful place beyond? I didn't know what to do. I looked at the beautiful place on the other side; I looked over at my family. I really wanted to go forward; it was so joyous and peaceful on the other side. Something deep inside me, however, prompted me to go back. It was as if I knew I had unfinished business to do in the world. I needed to go back; I wanted to be with my family. I would get another opportunity to venture over to that beautiful place. But for now, I knew I had to heed that small, still voice inside that was beckoning me to return home.

Chapter 21
The Fateful Car Accident

It had been seventeen days, and Will was still in a coma. So much time had gone by that many feared Will might never wake up; and if he did, they worried he'd never be the same. Claire refused to give into such fears. She decided right from the beginning that her son would wake up, and he would be just fine. Even with all she had been through, it was unlike her to ever give up hope.

Sitting next to his bed, Claire read her newspaper, and from time to time looked over at Will. She so desperately wanted to see his eyes open. *"Maybe today,"* she thought.

Reading the newspaper was something Claire loved to do. Each day she had a regular routine. On her way into the hospital, she bought a paper, and then went down to the hospital cafeteria to buy a cup of coffee. She then headed straight to Will's room. Each time she arrived, she relieved someone from Will's bedside. (It was very important to Claire that someone be with him at all times.) Between friends and family, Will was almost never left alone.

Claire read her newspaper out loud to Will. "In May, the Soviet Union shot down an American U-2 reconnaissance airplane over Soviet airspace and captured pilot Gary Powers, forcing U.S. to admit to aerial spying. Many wonder what will become of Mr. Powers and whether they will be able to bring him home." Claire was not always happy about what she read in the newspaper. More and more the papers seemed to be referring to the Soviet Union as a major threat to the United States and a country that wanted to see the demise of America.

Claire continued to read, "Studies linking cigarette smoking with heart disease." Adding her opinion, "I never thought cigarettes were safe. Inhaling tobacco is bound to harm our lungs and probably cause other terrible sicknesses." Will's comatose state put health at the forefront of her mind. Just yesterday, she and Lori were talking about life, and how too often people take it for granted. Being alive and well, and close to our loved ones was a blessing neither one of them would ever take for granted again.

Claire began to think about Lori. *"That sweet girl has been to the hospital every day to see Will. She is truly fond of him."* Lori and Claire had become close over the past seventeen days, enjoying each other's company. Lori talked about her dreams of becoming a doctor. If her grades continued to remain the same, she was hoping for a scholarship. Claire could see that Lori was a young girl with lofty and admirable goals.

During one of their conversations, Lori shared with Claire how her mom had encouraged her and assured her that dreams and goals were important. Lori's mom told her she could become anything she wanted. If becoming a doctor was what Lori wanted, then she needed to press on toward that goal. With tears building in her eyes, Lori said, "If it wasn't for my mom, I don't know if I would have ever had the courage to follow my dreams. She made me feel I could do anything." It was at that moment Lori began sharing the circumstances of her mother's death, explaining that it had been a little over two years since her mom, Katherine, died in a terrible car accident. Katherine had been driving home one evening after dropping Lori off at a friend's house. Lori remembered giving her mom a kiss and hug before getting out of the car. Her mom said her customary 'I love you' to Lori, and they each went on their way. It was obvious to Claire that Lori and her mom shared a remarkable bond of love, respect and friendship.

Being a military family, they moved around a lot, and because of that, Lori felt she never had the chance to make lasting friendships. She believed this was one of the reasons she and her mom became so close. Her dad had a demanding job that required a great deal of traveling. Due to his absence, Lori and her mom spent many evenings together, just the two of them. Their closeness made Katherine's death that much more traumatic and difficult for Lori.

Lori's account of the accident was difficult and painful. "My mom had just dropped me off at my friend, Jan's house. It was early evening. My dad said this was the time when visibility, while driving a car, was at its worst. Many believed this may have been one of the circumstances leading up to my mom's accident."

After a brief pause, Lori continued, "Between Jan's house and ours there is a very busy intersection, and it was at this intersection that my mom's car was hit. She had come to a stop and was waiting for the light to change. While sitting there, she must have seen the perilous beginning of what soon would take her life. Approaching to her right was a young man driving a red, Dodge pick-up truck, the kind with a huge front hood. The pick up was coming toward the intersection at normal speed, knowing his traffic light was green. In front of my mom, a deep-blue Studebaker was approaching. The Studebaker was not slowing down for the approaching red light. Mom must have known what was about to happen and knew she could not avoid being a part of this impending crash. The pick up and the Studebaker collided with such force that the front end of the Dodge was ripped completely off, sending the young man flying into the air. The impact caused him to die instantly. The Studebaker, after being slammed, ran into my mom's car head on. The impact sent my mom's car careening backward over a ravine. Her car came to rest in some pine trees below. The first responders said my mom died on impact. Amazingly, the guy in the Studebaker, the one responsible for the entire thing, survived. The sheriff told my dad the reason the guy in the Studebaker ran the red light was because he had been intoxicated. To this day, Dad is sure to remind me, and any friends of mine, that we are to never drive while drinking nor to get into a car with someone who has been drinking. In fact, before Dad would allow Will to take me out, he made sure Will was aware of his strict rules."

Once Lori finished telling her mom's story, she and Claire just sat in silence for what seemed a long time. Lori was the first to speak, remarking how strongly she believed that Will was going to wake up and be well again. They were in agreement about that.

Later, as Claire sat there thinking about all she and Lori talked about that day, she reached down and took hold of Will's hand. As she did, Will began to wiggle his fingers.

Chapter 22
Eyes Finally Open

Will was trying to wake up when he heard his mom calling him. She began to shout, "Will! Honey, it's me, Mom. Oh dear God, oh dear God! Will, honey can you hear me? It's Mom. Will, please wake up, please!"

Just then, Will's eyes slowly opened, and he looked around the room. Scowling as if the bright light of the hospital room were blinding him, in a barely audible whisper, Will began to speak, "Mom, where am I? What's going on?" Stunned and groggy, Will asked how long he'd been in that bed. "My head is pounding. Mom, what's going on?" Will was starting to remember all that had happened, the race, the accident and Sandy. "The accident!"

Will lifted his hand up to his forehead, and rubbed his hand over the top of his face. He was desperately trying to come to terms with what he remembered. "Where's Sandy, Mom? Is he okay? I remember the accident. Dear God in heaven! Do I ever remember the accident! I remember looking behind me, because Sandy and I were way ahead of everyone else, and having that rush of excitement, knowing we were going to finally win. And then we started to fall. Sandy stepped in a hole; I'm sure of it. I could have sworn I saw it just before we hit the ground."

Claire couldn't believe Will was able to remember all that had happened. "Will, Darling, you have been here in the hospital for quite a while. I'm going to grab the nurse; they need to see you right away. Please, be still, Will. In due time, we can talk about everything."

Claire ran out of the room, and quickly grabbed the first nurse she saw. She told her what happened. The nurse ran back to the room with Claire and was thrilled to see that Will had awoken. She shouted out to the nurse's station, "Call Dr. Halbig, right away. Will's awake! William Casey is awake!" Outside the room you could hear the clamor. Nurses were crying, clapping, and even laughing with overwhelming joy.

There were so many people Claire had to notify. "Nurse, I need to call Jonathan. May I use that phone over there, the one at your station?"

Happy to oblige, the nurse said, "Absolutely, Claire. Go right ahead. We really need to examine Will; so, you will have to stay out of the room for a little while anyway."

Claire reached Jonathan at the mill and told him the exciting news. Jonathan was so elated that tears began to stream down his face, and he didn't care who saw him. Tears and all, he ran out to the center of the mill, and told the guys the great news. The entire place was roaring and clapping. It was loud, and it was happy.

Susan answered the phone, and it was Jonathan relating the happy news. All she could do was cry and thank God. Claire had prepared a list of all the people she wanted to call when Will finally woke up. Susan offered to take care of that. After family members were called, the last three to be called were Lori, Bart and Gregg. Once Susan reached Lori, she barely had time to finish telling her the great news when Lori dropped the phone and ran out the door. Running as fast as she could, she headed for the hospital.

News travels fast in Kateyville, and soon most of the town new Will had awakened from his coma. The fact that Lori ran down Cayey Lane on her way to the hospital, shouting, "Will's awake! Will's awake!" to everyone she saw most likely had something to do with that. The news was met with lots of hootin' an' hollerin', as Harry used to like to say. It was a splendid day, to say the least.

Dr. Halbig arrived, and he was elated. "Well, well my young man. You decided to join the land of the living I see. How are you feeling? Do you remember what put you here in the first place?"

Looking at Dr. Halbig, Will broke out in a smile. He had always liked the man, and thought he was pretty humorous. Dr. Halbig had a great bedside manner, and he had a way of making most of his patients laugh, no matter what their circumstance. You couldn't help but feel at ease when he was taking care of you.

"Well, Doctor, I have a bit of a headache, and I'm starving, and yes, I know how I got here."

Dr. Halbig replied, "Headache and starving, you say? Those just happen to be two things I can fix." He called the nurse over, "Do me a favor Brenda. Will you go get Will something to eat? We'll start with a little jell-o and chicken broth, along with a cup of mushroom soup."

Will interrupted, "Oh, Dr. Halbig, I don't like mushroom soup."

Dr. Halbig laughed a bit and said, "That's good, because the soup's for me." The whole room started to laugh.

After Will ate his meal, the doctor wanted him to be left alone for a while. Even though Will had lots of questions, the doctor wanted him to rest. "Let him rest a bit, Claire. This will give me some time to tell you about what comes next for Will. Rehabilitation is going to be a long process. It's going to take months. He'll be able to handle it, I'm sure, but I don't want him getting impatient. He needs to understand that it's going to take time. I need you to assure him of that. If he understands right from the beginning, maybe he'll have more tolerance for the process."

Claire agreed.

Chapter 23
Lori Hears the News

Lori ran through the hospital doors and raced for the elevator. *Will's awake! Will's awake!* This was all that ran through her mind. Reaching the second floor, she ran as fast as she could toward Will's room. Nearly running into an older gentleman wheeling a cart full of flowers, she was apologetic. "Oh, I'm so sorry," were the words coming from her mouth as she turned to look back at the man, never slowing down, and almost running into another person.

The older gentlemen gave Lori a nasty look, and ranted, "Darn kids today!"

Finally, she reached Will's door. Claire and Dr. Halbig were standing outside having a conversation. Completely out of breath, all Lori could get out was, "Can I see him? Can I?"

Claire looked up at Dr. Halbig, "Come on Brad, you can't deny her this visit. Look how desperate she is to see him. He needs to see her too. I'll be sure to have him rest when she leaves."

Dr. Halbig was reluctant, but finally conceded, "Okay, Lori, but only for a little while." Lori never even said thank you; she just ran into Will's room.

As soon as Lori saw Will, tears welled up in her eyes.

Will looked at Lori with a smile that stretched clear across his face and said, "Hi, Lor; what took you so long?" He wore a look, which in a comical way, wanted to make light of his return.

Lori ran to his bedside and cradled his head in her hands, "Oh Will, I've missed you so much. I knew you'd wake up; I just knew it!" Lori gently pressed her lips to his, and they kissed. They embraced each other, and neither one of them wanted to let go. The familiar warmth they felt was incredibly comforting.

Lori found a chair next to Will's bed and sat down. After sitting, she grabbed Will's hand and just looked into his eyes for a very long time.

So much needed to be said and explained. There was still so much Will didn't know. Lori wasn't sure how prepared she would be for his questions. If Will asked her about Sandy, she didn't know what she would say. The last thing she wanted to do was lie to Will, but the one thing Susan told Lori was, "Please don't tell Will about Sandy. Gregg wants to be the one to tell him. He was there with Sandy during his final moments, and Gregg wants to explain everything." And Lori had agreed. It made perfect sense to her.

"How long have I been here?" Will asked.

Lori looked at Will with compassion, "Will, have you talked to your mom? Did she tell you anything? How much do you remember?"

Will responded, "Mom and I haven't really talked much. She just said that it had been a long time, and lots of people have been praying for me."

Lori took a deep breath and answered Will. "Seventeen days...you've been unconscious for seventeen days. Some people didn't know if you would ever wake up, but your mom and I...we never doubted it."

"I've been out seventeen days? I guess I scared you guys a bit. What happened after the accident? I just remember turning around to see the horses behind us and then falling, spitting out dirt, and then nothing. Sandy...he was laying on top of me; and he was hurt. He couldn't move, and I felt like I couldn't breathe. What happened to Sandy? What happened to him after the accident? Please tell me he's all right, Lori!" Will was unrelenting; he peppered Lori with some pretty heavy questions.

Lori knew Will wanted to know what happened to Sandy, but she couldn't tell him; she'd promised. Instead, she did her best to draw his attention away from Sandy by answering some of his other questions first. She began by telling him what had been going on at school. Will could have stopped her by demanding to know about Sandy, but he didn't, maybe because of fear and an ominous feeling that he wasn't ready to hear the truth about what had happened to his best friend. In his heart, he was already beginning to fear the worst.

Lori decided to 'play it down', not wanting him to think he had missed very much. "Not a lot has happened, really, nothing too significant anyway." That was her first lie, and she knew it. She continued, "The greatest news has been Susan's pregnancy. On Sunday, she and Jonathan told everyone."

Will chimed in, "By the way, what day is it today?"

"Today is Wednesday, August twenty-fourth," Lori said with a bit of a languished look that revealed how badly she felt for Will; she knew this was all so overwhelming for him. Lori continued, "And let me see, what else…Oh, many people have been saying that if John Kennedy beats Richard Nixon in this year's election, he might be the most handsome President we've ever had. I think they're right!"

Will jumped in, "Hey, have you been looking at other guys?" They both began to laugh.

Lori searched for other topics. "Oh, the hottest movie out right now is *Psycho*. I told Rebecca there was no way I would see it without you." Lori started to chuckle a bit, "So, once you're up and around, maybe we can go?"

Lori told Will about all the new groovy songs she had been hearing on the radio. Songs like; *Itsy Bitsy Teeny Weenie Yellow Polka Dot Bikini, Let's Do the Twist, Teen Angel* and her favorite song, *Are You Lonesome Tonight* by Elvis Presley. She told Will that whenever she heard that song she thought of him. "I kind of made it *our* song, Will."

With a sad look on his face, "I'm sorry I made you worry. I know this hasn't been easy for you." He squeezed her hand, and romantically spoke, "I don't want you to be lonely anymore."

Trying to lighten things up a bit, Will gave Lori a wink and asked her, "I know you love to read. What books have you been reading?

"Well," Lori responded, "I've read quite a few, but my absolute favorite is *The Citadel* by A.J. Cronin. If you think you'll feel like reading it, I'll bring it to you tomorrow. It will give you something to do. I'm not sure how long you're going to be here."

With a deep breath and a sigh, Will responded, "I hope not long. I need to see Sandy. I don't think they'll let him in here, do you?"

Lori stammered for words. She couldn't bring herself to be dishonest anymore. She needed to tell him. "Something sad happened while you were unconscious, Will."

Will, nervous for an answer, responded, "What, Lori?"

Lori quickly changed her mind. "Um, I read somewhere that Clark Gable is really sick, and they think he may die."

Almost relieved, Will spoke, "Oh, that's too bad."

Lori couldn't stand this any longer. She couldn't lie to Will anymore, "Will, Something else happened, something…"

Lori was interrupted by a knock on the door. Lori turned around. It was Dr. Halbig asking to see her. She gave Will a kiss, and told him to rest. She promised that she'd be back later. Once leaving the room, Lori saw Gregg Pace standing with Claire. She knew what was finally coming. Will wouldn't be lied to anymore, but unfortunately, now, his heart was about to be broken.

Chapter 24
Will's Heartbreak

Slowly, Gregg opened the door to Will's room, and then quietly closed it. Will was resting his eyes, and didn't hear him come in. As Gregg got close to his bed, Will opened his eyes, and with a trace of grogginess, he whispered, "Hey, Gregg. How are ya?"

Gregg gave a smile, "How am I? How are you, Buddy? You took quit a long nap."

"So they say," Will chuckled.

This wasn't going to be easy. Gregg knew it, but Will needed to know what happened. He began by asking Will if he remembered the accident. "You were both banged up pretty bad. We didn't think either of you were going to make it. After the ambulance took you away, we started to move Sandy. He was in real bad shape, Will, real bad."

Will didn't like the feeling he was getting. "How bad, Gregg? How bad was he hurt?"

Gregg looked at Will with regret in his eyes. "He couldn't pick up his head, Will. His neck was broken."

Tears were now welling up in both their eyes, and as one found its way down Will's cheek, he asked Gregg what he didn't want to know. "Where's Sandy, Gregg? What happened to him? Lori never said…"

Gregg interrupted, "I wanted to be the one to tell you, Will. Lori respected that. I was with Sandy when he…He knew you loved him, Will, and that beautiful horse, he loved you too. He was suffering. We needed to put him at peace. Dr. Brown was there, and she didn't want to do what she knew she had to. Before Dr. Brown administered the medication, I held him in my arms, and I told him how much you loved him, how much we all loved him. I held on tight, and I never left his side until our eyes said that final goodbye."

In Will's memory it seemed only yesterday he had been with Sandy. He felt overwhelmed; thoughts were spinning around in his head. Will needed time to come to terms with all that had happened. He was living a nightmare; losing seventeen days of his life, and losing Sandy was too much for him. He couldn't look at Gregg; he turned his head to face the window. Looking away wasn't because he blamed Gregg; Will knew how much Gregg loved Sandy. He was sure none of this came easy for him, but right now, he just needed to be alone. With tears falling to the pillow, Will asked Gregg if he could be alone.

Gregg understood, "Sure Will. You have a lot to get used to, and I know it's not going to be easy. I wish things could have been different. I'm sorry, Will. I'm really sorry."

Will had one final question, "Where's Sandy now?"

Gregg closed his eyes for a moment, and then explained to Will what happened to Sandy after they put him to sleep. "I gave Sandy's ashes to your mom. She asked that he be cremated. I'm really sorry, Will. Nobody wanted to let Sandy go." And with that, Gregg left the room.

Will just stared at the ceiling. Gregg's disclosure was devastating and left Will feeling crushed and empty.

Chapter 25
Just Stay Away

The hospital was now clamoring with friends and family who wanted to see Will. Susan brought the boys, Christopher and Lenny. Bart and Shannon arrived together. They pleaded with Dr. Halbig to allow them to just say a quick hello to Will.

In a very cautionary tone, Dr. Halbig said he would ask Will, and if Will wanted to see them for just a little while, ten minutes tops, it would be fine with him.

Dr. Halbig entered Will's room, and began talking to him. "This is quite a day you've had, my young man. There are quite a few people outside that would like to see you. Are you up for a very short visit, or would you like to rest?"

Will never turned to look at the doctor. Instead, he just stared out the window.

Dr. Halbig spoke up, "Will? Shannon's outside, and so is Bart and the boys. Jonathan and Susan are here too."

Will choked out his response. "No, I don't want to see anyone!" Hiding his tears, he whispered, "Tell them to go!"

Devastation was only a fraction of what he was feeling now. So many other emotions were clamoring for space in his head. He had feelings of loss, loneliness, regret and utter sadness, and he had many more questions. *What went wrong? How could this have happened? God, are you finished pummeling me yet? How much more do I have to go through? Who else are you going to take away from me? Well, I'll tell ya what, No one! I'm not getting close to another soul.*

Entering the hallway where everyone stood, Dr. Halbig informed everyone that Will was resting and didn't want to see anyone. He assured them that in the morning Will would feel more like having visitors. Dr. Halbig encouraged everyone to go home, get some rest, and check back with him tomorrow.

Understandably, everyone was disappointed, and Claire was reluctant to leave. She knew Gregg told Will about Sandy, and she was worried about him. After a great deal of coaxing, Claire eventually acquiesced. This had been a remarkable day, to say the least, and she was sure Will was very tired.

Chapter 26
Nurse Thelma

I couldn't believe Sandy was gone. The pain I felt over losing Sandy was in so many ways comparable to the pain I felt when losing Dad and Sarah—an overwhelming feeling of loss, a feeling of hopelessness. The realization of all that had happened finally hit me. I didn't care if I ever got out of that bed.

After a lull in the noise coming from the hallway, things started to pick up again. Phones were ringing, messages were coming from the speakers, and carts were being shuffled along with the clamor of fast feet. The next thing I knew, a nurse entered my room. She was a dark skinned woman who, even though was probably in her mid-fifties, didn't have one wrinkle on her kind-looking face. She was a substantial woman, and it wasn't long before I discovered she was a bold talker as well. Holding onto the clipboard file she had taken from the plastic pocket hanging on the outside of my room, she began to wave her pen around in the air. "Hello, hello young man. I see you decided to wake up today. Well, it's about time, don't you think?"

Ignoring her, I never made a sound. Instead, I just lay there, looking out the window, reminding myself that I wanted the shade shut before morning came. I made a mental note to tell the nurse. The sunrise was something I no longer wanted any part of.

"Has the cat got your tongue? I said hello, Sweetheart! My name is Nurse Thelma, and I'm going to be taking care of you for the next twelve hours. It's time you got yourself up and out of that bed. Don't you worry; I have some help coming. Now, this isn't going to be easy;

you have a long row to hoe ahead of you. You're gonna have to just hang tight and let that progress come to you in small doses each day. Don't rush it, and don't be impatient. You'll be back to normal eventually; you'll see."

Normal? I think *I'll never be back to normal.* "Hello, Thelma. I'm Will, William Casey." Speaking with no enthusiasm whatsoever, I suppose I sounded as depressed as I felt.

Thelma thought to herself, *Boy, oh, boy. This boy's been through the ringer. It's gonna take a strong man to pull himself up and outa this one. Dear Lord, give this young man strength. He's gonna really need You now. His mama is really worried about him. I promised her I'd take good care of him, and now I'm asking You for some help.*

A male nurse came into the room with some crutches and a walker. Thelma shouted out with eagerness, "Look who we have here. It's Nurse Paul. He's gonna help me get you outa bed. Are you ready, Will? Well, ready or not here we go."

The last thing I wanted to do was talk, and I sure didn't want to see if my legs worked. "I don't know, Thelma. Maybe tomorrow."

With a sarcastic chuckle, "Nope, you're doing it now." She made it perfectly clear that I had no choice; there was no arguing with *this* nurse.

As I looked at Nurse Paul, I couldn't believe how big he was. *Who is this guy, a heavy weight champion? This guy's huge. He's got arms like Popeye.*

The first thing the nurses did was get on both sides of my bed, and then they slowly sat me up. I felt a bit lightheaded as they told me I probably would. "How ya doing, Will? Are you a little dizzy?" Thelma asked.

I had to admit that I was a bit dizzy. Not only that, I had a headache, a big one.

Thelma assured me, "You just sit tight. We're not going to move too fast. When your dizziness calms down, we'll move you over to the side of your bed. Okay?"

Eventually, my legs were dangling over the side of my bed. It was then I rather embarrassingly realized my backside was exposed. *Oh this*

130

is great; I can't stand up like this. I need a robe or something. Who designed these stupid things anyway? All open in the back like that! "Um, Thelma, do you have a robe I could put on? I'm kinda cold back there, if you know what I mean."

Thelma chuckled, "Sure, but listen, I'm old enough to be your mama, so don't go getting yourself all embarrassed. Now, wait just a minute, and I'll go get ya one."

Looking down at my legs, I could see how banged up they were. Both were smattered with tracks of stitches, gashes and a few black-and-blue marks that I swore looked like the shape of a horseshoe. Looking at my injuries had a way of bringing back memories of the accident. Thinking back, I remembered hearing the other riders yelling and screaming, trying not to hit us, but it looks like they had no choice. I knew it was pretty amazing I survived such an accident; I just wish that Sandy could have been as fortunate. Surviving without Sandy makes it hard to celebrate; in fact, it stinks.

After a few minutes, Thelma let me back down in my bed. The sheets had been changed, and they smelled clean and fresh, a bit like home. An hour later, Thelma came back with my dinner and demanded that I eat.

After a slight protest, explaining that I had already eaten a little while ago, she informed me she wasn't listening to any excuses and told me to eat. "You need to build up your strength. You're gonna have to stand a whole lot longer tomorrow, and food's gonna help you do that."

After she left, I stared at overcooked vegetables, instant potatoes, canned applesauce and some kind of meat that wasn't easily distinguishable. I lamented that it wasn't anything like Mom's cooking. Thinking about Mom's meals started to make me sad all over again. Anytime I had thoughts of the past, the memories would bring me right back to recollections of Sandy. Pushing my meal aside, I wondered how I was ever going to carry on without my friend.

Chapter 27
Seclusion

For many days, as I wallowed in gloom and misery, I allowed only my mother into my hospital room. I told Thelma, and any other nurse caring for me, not to let anyone else in, and because I was eighteen, I was sure that I could set the ground rules for such visits. Mom wasn't happy. She said I was hurting the people who loved and cared for me, and it was unnecessary.

That's exactly what she didn't understand. It was necessary. Let's face it; the people I love don't always stick around. I couldn't bring myself to love another human being, or animal, so completely ever again. The ones I do love, well, I'm going to keep them at a distance. Soon the feelings would fade, and living without them wouldn't be so hard. In my mind, I felt it was the sensible thing to do. Why put myself through more potential and painful grief?

Shutting my mom out would have been cruel; I knew that much. She had been through each tragic loss with me. The loss of Dad was doubly unjust and painful for her. Besides, no one deserved to be widowed at such a young age, especially my mom. I promised my dad I would take care of her, and I meant it.

With each day of my rehabilitation, I was getting stronger and stronger. Thanks to Thelma's unrelenting determination, I was finally able to move around without help. I was relieved that I hadn't had a headache in at least a week. During one of my regular ventures outside my hospital room, I was surprised to look up to see Bart walking towards me. Realizing he was one of the people I wouldn't allow to visit me, I knew I had to turn around and make a 'b-line' for my room. Moving fast was not going to be easy.

I had been shutting Bart out of my life since the accident, and even though he had been my friend since kindergarten, I didn't want to see him. I couldn't bear listening to him try to cheer me up. The best I could do was *pretend* to be happy, and that was just too much work for me right then.

Bart saw me just as I thought I was out of his eyeshot. "Will, stop! I mean it Will. Stop, or I'm going to run you down. Then you will have to start all this rehab business all over again!" Bart was angry and unwavering; he was insistent that I talk to him.

I shouted back at him, "Go away, Bart! I don't want to see you!"

It was no use. By the time I made it back to my hospital room door, Bart was in front of me. "We're going to talk! We're going to talk right now." It was clear to me that Bart was not going to back down.

"Fine, Bart. If you want to talk, we'll talk. You have five minutes!" I wasn't very nice, but I truly believed I was doing the best thing for myself.

We both took a seat in my room. Bart started talking, "Will, you and I have been friends for nearly our entire lives. I'm not going to go away easily. I know you hate the world right now. This world seems to be stripping you of everything you love. I understand that. If I were you, I don't know how I would react, maybe the same way. All I know is that you're like a brother to me, and I don't think any amount of time we spend apart will weaken the bond you and I share. You can go on kidding yourself, pretending you feel differently, but I know better! I was just hoping I could be here for you, to help you get through all this, the way we have always been there for each other in the past. But if you really want to end our friendship, I won't stop you. I love you like a brother, but I'm not going to force myself into your life." Bart got up and started to walk out of the room, and then he turned around to say one more thing. "I miss Sandy. He was a great horse and a great friend to you. When I think of him, my heart aches something terrible; so, I can't even begin to imagine your grief. I'm really sorry, Will."

Just as Bart was about to leave, I called him back into the room. As

I stretched out my hand in a gesture of apology, he extended his. Shaking hands, I asked him to forgive my bullheadedness. "I'm sorry, Bart. I'm a mess inside, and I just didn't know how to face anyone, even you. It's like my heart's gone hard, part from grief and part because I've wanted it to. I know I'm running from all emotion, but for the time being I simply don't know what else to do. I'm not the same, and if you can accept that, at least for now, then maybe…well, maybe it's a start."

The truth was, I didn't want to lose him as a friend, but expressing that was out of the question. Like a true friend, Bart graciously accepted my plea for leniency, and I was grateful. Amazingly, he visited me every day thereafter, helping me with my rehab. He is a genuine friend. I vowed I would never turn my back on him again.

It wasn't much longer before I was finally able to leave the hospital. I was anxious to get home. Bart, on the other hand, was worried about further adjustments and changes that I would be confronted with when I arrived home. He was at the hospital that morning ready and anxious to lend his support. He told me to take things one day at a time; so, that's what I intended to do.

Chapter 28
Mom's Warning

Bart never missed an opportunity to say something about Lori during those last few days in the hospital. He was hoping I would change my mind and agree to see her. "She really misses you, Will. She's willing to wait for you, hoping you'll change your mind. She's a great girl; you'd be crazy to let her go."

I was steadfast, "Bart, I can't. She needs to get on with her life and find someone else. I'm no good for her. Besides, I don't know where my life is headed anymore. Riding is out of the question, and so is the rodeo. I never thought about doing something else with my life, but now I have to. How can I even think about any type of commitment to someone else when I don't even know where I'm going myself?"

Bart countered, "Why can't you just take it one day at a time? Tell her you'll see her. At least talk to her. If after meeting with her, you still feel the same, intent on ending it, then so be it. I'll leave you alone. But I can't sit by and see both of you so miserable without trying to help the situation. You owe her that much, Will, and you know it."

I finally understood why it was so important to Bart that Lori and I talk. He was not only my friend, but he had become her friend, as well. He didn't like seeing her hurt. Honestly, I didn't either, but my mind was made up. "Bart, just leave this alone, please. I'm not going to see her, and that's that!"

Since my conversation with Bart, I was finding myself thinking about Lori a great deal. The thought of her being sad because of me was really playing on my mind, and I would be lying if I said I didn't miss her. The fact is, as hard as I tried, I couldn't seem to get her out of my head. I really thought that if we stayed apart from each other, our love would fade, and we could each move on. Truthfully, I knew if I saw her, I would probably crumble, and I just couldn't take that chance. An abrupt end to our relationship seemed to be my only option.

My cynicism was unfortunate, but I felt it was a much better choice than possibly ruining two lives. When I explained this reasoning to Bart, he told me that my fears were pretty unrealistic. I suppose he could have been right, but the sad reality was that I had lost hope for the future, and any hope of something lasting with Lori. Besides, I had a track record of losing those I cared too much about. My mind wouldn't let me see it any other way. Sure, my heart wanted things to be different, to have a future with her. But given all that had happened, I was afraid to believe that it could be a reality. Loving her and having a relationship with her was much too dangerous. In some crazy way, I believed that if I allowed myself to care too much for her, it would only serve to set myself up for another loss, just as I had lost Sarah, Dad and Sandy. I didn't want to endure anything like that, ever again.

During my stay in the hospital, Mom brought in several letters Lori had written and delivered to the house. She feared that if she sent them to the hospital, I would just destroy them without reading them. Again and again, I told my mom to throw them away. Mom said she couldn't do that, and that one day she hoped I would read them. Each time she took the letters back home with her. Slowly, my mother began to lose patience with me. I could tell she no longer enjoyed trying to be so accommodating. In the beginning, just after the accident, she felt sorry for me. She knew losing Sandy put me in a fragile state and thought at the time it was better not to push. But sooner or later, I knew she would start to see things differently. My mom was a sweet and compassionate woman, but she had her limits. This I knew for sure.

It had been quite a while since I arrived home from the hospital, and I hadn't been very productive. I shuffled around the house bored and feeling depressed. I didn't want to go outside. I didn't want to look at the barn; I didn't want to be reminded of Sandy, and sure as anything, I didn't want to remember those morning sunrises spent with Dad and him. Watching the sunrise was no longer a pleasant ritual, but rather an event to be left in the past. Each night before bed, I made sure to pull my shade.

Mom stood by and took careful note of my antics and downcast demeanor, and by the end of week two, she had had enough! "William, I need to talk to you. Please come and sit at the table with me. You and I need to have a talk!"

There was something in her tone. She had something serious to say, and I knew it was useless to try to avoid the conversation. I sat down.

"Mom, what is it? What do you need to talk to me about?" I was cautiously curious.

"Your behavior is causing me great concern. I can't sit by and just watch. You have hurts and fears; this I understand, but your life must go on. Is this the way your father would have wanted you to live? You barely speak with your little brothers, Christopher and Lenny. You avoid Shannon every chance you get, and you never return Jonathan's phone calls. Did you even notice how much time Shannon and Bart have been spending together? I dare say that you haven't, because you are completely absorbed in your own pain and grief, and no one else seems to matter to you anymore. Is this the kind of son we raised? All those years you spent with your father, listening to his advice, admiring his character and trying to be just like him, and this is what has become of it?" Mom was dishing out some tough love.

I didn't know what to say. "Mom, I…"

She interrupted, "Do you even know what Lori has been up to? In spite of the hurt you've caused her, she continues to keep you in mind while making plans for her future. She has not lost sight of her dream of going to medical school. And do you know what? She has been accepted by three different universities to begin pre-med studies this fall. She has been offered scholarships to St. Lawrence University, University of Buffalo and NY University. If she attends St. Lawrence University, she knows she will be close to you, just over in the next town. If she accepts NYU's offer, she will be clear down in New York City, and UB will also take her far away from you. What do you really want, Will? I believe that if you continue to push her away, you may lose her. Is that truly what you want?

"You are both young and have a lot of living to do. She is a dear friend, and it would be nice if you would encourage her and wish her well no matter where she chooses to go to school. She seems so right for you. If it is meant to be, and after you have matured and pursued your ambitions, possibly there will be a future for the two of you. No one knows exactly what the future holds, but you need to remember what a devoted and loving friend she and many others have been in the past. Would it hurt to wish her well as she begins her studies?"

I coldly responded, "I want Lori to do whatever she wants. I've made my choice. It's over between us."

Mom couldn't believe her ears. "I am not talking about a relationship, Will. I'm talking about a friendship. I hope you're sure about what you're doing, because if you're not, you're running out of time."

Deep in my mom's heart, she knew I was lying to myself.

Chapter 29
Making the Wrong Choice

I decided to take a long, hot shower, and then do my best to figure out what I was going to do with my life. The whole idea of facing what lay ahead frightened me to death. Jonathan called and wanted me to stop by the mill; he thought maybe I would enjoy working there. I told him I would be there sometime this morning, and we could talk about it. After leaving the house and before going to the mill, I decided to go check out the town for a bit, see what was happening.

It was Saturday, and Cayey Lane was bustling with lots of activity. The October air was mild with the lingering scent of fallen leaves, fresh cut grass, and the ripe smell of Mr. Bailey's dairy farm. Everything around me made me feel glad I was home again. As I walked down the street, I nearly passed by Mr. Dune's recruitment center before I saw who was there. I saw Lori through the front window. My heart began to beat rapidly, and I felt as though my feet were frozen to the pavement. Her silhouette momentarily consumed my entire focus. Seeing her, brought to the surface feelings I was desperately trying to bury.

As I looked through the window, I could see her long blond hair fall softly over her petite shoulders until it reached the center of her back. A pastel blue cardigan tapered her tiny waist, and a navy blue plaid skirt rested just below her knees. On her feet, she wore ankle socks and light blue suede shoes to match her sweater. She appeared to be dressed for something special. I felt as if I couldn't take my eyes off her, but I knew I had to get out of there.

Just as I found the strength to leave, I noticed a tall, rather handsome gentlemen enter the recruitment center. He walked up to Lori, gave her a hug, and a small kiss on the cheek. I was instantly overcome with strong feelings of jealousy! Confusing and conflicting emotions were rising up within me. A couple of years ago, I probably would have gone up to the guy and demanded that he stay away from my girl. Doing something like that now would only make things worse; Lori would think I had gone completely mad.

Common sense said that the right thing for me to do would be to walk away. After all, I was the one who had ended things between Lori and me, and I deserved the fall out. So, walk away, right? No. Not me. I couldn't.

Chapter 30
Embarrassed and Regretful

There was a park bench outside Mr. Dune's recruitment center, and before I knew what was happening, I found myself seated there. I figured Lori would be leaving soon, and I decided I would sit there until she did. As soon as she and this guy walked out, I would say hello and introduce myself to her new friend.

Oh boy, before I knew it, they walked out the door and almost right passed me. I stood up and blurted out, "Hello, Lori."

Lori would have walked completely passed me if I hadn't risen from the bench when I did. She was stunned and didn't know what to say.

I began to speak rather boldly, "Aren't you going to say hello?"

Lori looked at me with confusion in her eyes, and I could tell she was trying to make sense of our meeting. We hadn't spoken in over a month, so all she could say was, "Hi, Will."

Curiosity was getting the best of me, "Who's your friend? Are you going to introduce us?"

Suddenly, I could tell that Lori now understood what this was about. Looking at me with eyes filled with disappointment and hurt, she said, "No, Will. I don't think I will introduce you. I hope you're doing well. Have a nice day." Lori's response was curt and flat. Afterward, she simply walked away.

After Lori walked away, I knew I had created quite a quagmire for myself, and I wasn't feeling too good about it either.

I never made it to the mill; instead, I walked around town a bit and then headed out to Bart's house. When I got there, Bart wasn't home. His mom said he and Shannon drove to nearby Vermont to see the foliage.

After I left Bart's house, I began to think about what his mom said. She told me he and Shannon were together. They were together in Vermont? Mom said something about them, but I didn't care enough to ask. Bart was right about me. Since the accident and Sandy's death, I have been acting like a jerk, full of myself and only doing what I thought was best for me. I wondered what else I had missed, and what else I had probably lost.

While in my coma, I had a dream. Walking back home, I started to think about certain aspects of that dream. Obviously, the dream represented a critical choice I had to make, a decision to die or stay among the living. I chose to stay and live, but I certainly hadn't acted that way since I came out of the coma. I haven't been experiencing life as I should. I was given a second chance, and I was blowing it. I have pushed away nearly everyone who has ever meant anything to me, the people who have stuck by me and didn't give up on me.

Back at the house, I decided it was time I made my way down to Sandy's barn. It wouldn't be easy; I knew that, but I had to start facing the realities of my life. Sandy was gone, and he wasn't coming back.

The closer I got to the barn, various aromas began to spark memories from the past. The invigorating, yet soothing, scent of hay invaded my senses. As I opened the barn doors and stepped inside, I could see several bales of hay I had stacked next to Sandy's stall. After entering Sandy's stall, I sat on the floor, closed my eyes, and imagined him there with me. Reminiscent of the past, I took in the smell of stale manure, horse fur and liniment. The pungent, yet pleasant, smell of grain brought back memories of my many, earlier visits to the barn.

Words couldn't describe my loneliness and grief. Hardening my heart after the accident was my way of not facing Sandy's death; I realize that now. Sandy deserved more than that. The problem was that I had no idea how I would ever be able to say goodbye. I sat there in that world that was once ours, and I could no longer control my grief or the utter loneliness inside me that ached for his presence. Broken and sad, I bowed my head, with my palms pressed up against my forehead, and began to cry.

Chapter 31
The Truth about Sarah

Mom saw me walk up to the house from the barn, and I knew she was curious about what had transpired that day. She called out from the porch, "Will, Jonathan is on the phone. He said you didn't show up today. He would like to know why?"

I suppose I had some explaining to do. Jonathan didn't like to be stood up, and he was most certainly a man of punctuality. I shouted back to Mom, "Would you tell him I'm heading over there right now, and ask him to please wait for me. I will explain everything when I get there. Okay?"

Mom said she would do that for me. I knew she was wondering herself why I hadn't shown up at the mill, but she didn't ask. Come to think of it, "trial by fire" was one of her favorite sayings. I think she was trying to say that the difficulties of life are worth the pain if we learn valuable lessons. More often than not, she explained, good things develop out of hardship. Having said that, going through my own trials, I appreciate her words more than ever, and I think I finally understand her reasoning. You could say that all those imparted words of wisdom both she and Dad often gave are finally having some effect. If I could get through the present doldrums, the heartache of losing Sandy and my shattered relationship with Lori, I would be stronger and wiser. I was sure of it.

I quickly ran into the house to thank Mom for delivering my message and told her I would be back as soon as I could.

Once I made it to the mill, most everyone was gone, except a couple of guys scheduled for the night shift. Jonathan was standing in the front door with an obvious look of displeasure on his face.

"I want to explain, Jonathan; thanks for waiting. I'm sorry I didn't make it to the mill today. I don't have a suitable excuse, but I do have something I need to talk to you about. Could we talk?"

Curious and concerned, Jonathan spoke, "We can talk in my office. It will be more private there."

"Thanks, Jonathan." Seeing the look on his face when I arrived, made me feel even worse for not getting there earlier. He clearly looked let down and unhappy. His displeasure in me was something that was a consequence I had to accept.

Once inside his office and the door closed, I began. "Jonathan, I'm not sure where to begin. I guess I've finally realized that I have been treating everyone pretty bad since the accident, and I'm really sorry about that."

Jonathan looked at me with one eyebrow raised, as if to say, "You just realized this?"

I explained myself, "Well, I knew I was treating everyone pretty bad, but I tried not to care. Now, I do. I could only think of myself and my own loss—never mind anyone else's."

After a short pause, I continued, "I wouldn't allow myself to see the pain everyone experienced after the accident. You all feared that I might die, and you were sad about Sandy. You all loved Sandy too. I've been indulging myself, only willing to believe I was the only one suffering. I have been selfish; I realize that now, and I'm sorry."

Jonathan nodded, as though to say he understood.

I shared more, "After Sandy died, something inside me died too. Along with the sadness, I felt anger, a lot of it. This family of ours has been dealing with death ever since Sarah died, and in my mind, it has been my fault."

Jonathan tried to discount my guilt, "None of this has been your fault, Will."

Insistently, I continued, "I never told anybody what happened that day, the day Sarah died. I want to tell you."

144

Jonathan looked deeply concerned, "Okay, Will, go ahead; I'm listening."

Tears began to fill my eyes, and I feared I wouldn't be able to say what I needed to say without breaking down, but I pressed on. "It's my fault Sarah drowned that day. I was on my way to go swimming; she begged me to take her along. I didn't want her to go with me. I just wanted to hang out with my friends and not be bothered, but Mom insisted I take her.

"I remember what Mom said, 'Just let her take a dip to cool off, Will, and then bring her back. It's been so sticky lately; she's been really hot. You can hang out with your friends later.'

"I wasn't happy about it, but I took Sarah with me. I complained the whole way to the swimming hole. Walking beside me, she tried to hold my hand, but I wouldn't let her. She stared up at me with those big blue eyes of hers, and I could see tears collecting in the corners. I still wouldn't hold her hand!"

I had to stop. Placing my elbows on my knees, and then putting my hands up to my face, I started to cry. "I can't believe how mean I was to Sarah that day. If I'd only known…"

Jonathan sat quietly, careful not to interrupt.

Slowly, composing myself, I continued, "Once we got to the water hole, Sarah asked me to go swimming with her. She wanted me to throw her up in the air like I always did. She loved that! I'd toss her up, and then with a big splash, she'd land in the water in front of me.

"I told her, no. I wanted to talk to my friends first. I never saw her get into the water."

With tears now streaming down my face, I continued. "I turned around to check on her, and I couldn't find her. Screaming her name, I panicked! After I jumped in the water, I frantically searched the bottom for her. My three friends did the same. The water was so dark we couldn't see a thing, so all we could do was feel around with our hands, praying to God we would touch her, and get to her before it was too late. I remember touching the murky bottom, my hands sinking into the black mud. Almost running out of air, I came to the surface, exhaled, took in a deep breath and then dove back down. This seemed to go on forever, and with every passing minute my panic escalated. Somehow, I knew she was down there somewhere. I knew if I didn't find her soon, she would never make it. Finally, my hand touched her! I lifted her lifeless body to the surface and swam with her to the shore. I tried everything I knew to bring her back, but I couldn't. She wouldn't wake up! I screamed at God to please help me. Those beautiful blue eyes never opened. I knew right then and there that I killed her; it was my fault."

Jonathan got up from his chair and with tears in his eyes, knelt down next to Will and held him. As he hugged him, he said, "Will, you were just a normal kid. I know you feel responsible, but you didn't kill Sarah. It was an accident, just a horrible, horrible accident."

Once I was able to stop crying, I told Jonathan that I wasn't finished; I had more to say.

Jonathan told me, "If you want, Will; I'm listening. I'm here for you, but none of this is necessary…"

I interrupted, "Please, Jonathan, I have to do this." I cleared my throat and began again, "The day Dad died, he was on his way to the race, to see me. He had never missed one of my races before. Maybe that was playing on his mind, but he was running late. Maybe he was running late, and so he hurried around so much that he never saw that truck coming. I'm sure that's what must have happened. I can't get it out of my head that his death is somehow my fault, too."

Jonathan tried to reassure Will that their dad's death was just an accident. Like Sarah, it was an accident. "Will, you can not blame yourself for what happened to Dad. None of that was your fault. It was the owner of that cement truck, that's whose fault it was, not yours! Jack's Cement Company broke the law the day they let that truck out on the road. They knew that pipe was sticking out way too far; it was illegal and dangerous, but they were too cheap to fix it! Fault lies with them!"

"I understand that, but it happened because of me. He rushed because of me."

Jonathan chimed in, "You're wrong, Will."

Continuing on, I attempted to explain, "Even though I felt Dad's death was my fault, Sandy helped me get through it. He had a way of comforting me and helping me forget my pain. He was more than a horse; he was my friend.

I continued, "Honestly, I felt responsible for Sandy's death too. He was my responsibility, and I let him die on the track."

Jonathan couldn't understand Will's reasoning, "Come on, Will. Why would that be your fault?"

I explained, "Sandy was acting a bit nervous before getting into the gate, like he knew something. I didn't listen to him. I figured it was just the huge crowd of people that got him acting all antsy. If I took the time to listen to him, took a look at the track, maybe none of that would have happened. Who knows?

"Seeing Lori today made me realize how much I was giving up, just by living with all this guilt. I know now that I have to give up feeling this way, and look toward the future with hope and purpose. I can't keep running from ghosts, Jonathan. Instead, I need to face them."

"Let us help you do that, Will."

I nodded.

Then, Jonathan wondered about Lori, "You saw Lori today? How'd that go?"

With a tone of disappointment in my voice, I responded, "It didn't go well at all. It appears she has found someone new, a tall good-looking guy, at that. I also made a complete fool of myself."

Jonathan hadn't heard that Lori found someone new. He was surprised.

Before I left, I had one more thing to say to Jonathan, "Jonathan, I've decided to do a couple of things, and I wanted to let you know what they are. First of all, I won't be needing a job. I'm going to race again. Somehow, someway I'm going to follow my dream. Second, I'm going to find those foals Mom said Sandy sired. I want 'em, Jonathan. I want them to be here with us."

"Lastly, I'm going to go see Lori. I realize it's probably too late for us, but I owe her an apology. I know I hurt her really bad, and it's about time I do what I can to fix that. It's important she know I still value her as a friend."

I sat thinking about Lori for a brief moment, and then I continued. "I know all about her own dreams. No matter how we go about reaching our dreams, I want to be her friend through it all. I love her, Jonathan, and if I can't have her as 'my girl', I want to at least have her as a friend."

Pondering what the future could be, I finished what I had to say, "The future is a mystery, Jonathan, but one I must go after." Feeling slightly optimistic, "And who knows, maybe I'll just marry her someday. If she'll have me, that is."

Seeing my openness, Jonathan asked, "Will, do you remember my senior year?"

"Yeah, I remember you as the star receiver for the football team. The papers were saying that you jumped farther and ran faster than any guy in the league. They said your future looked bright. I also remember you were dating Linda Andrews. She used to 'babysit' me."

Jonathan nodded, "During the finals of our football season, our team was scheduled to play Saranac High. Saranac High was undefeated and the best team in the league. A week before the game was to take place; University of California told Dad they wanted me after I graduated. All that was left to do was see how I played against one of the best football teams to be found at the high school level. The college scout told Dad that he saw no reason why we wouldn't be 'shaking hands' after that game. All I had to do was play like I knew I could."

Jonathon continued, "Before the game, I headed downtown to Kateyville Jewelers. I had been saving to buy Linda an engagement ring that whole year. I took the money I saved, and I bought her the nicest diamond I could get. Before the game, in the locker room, I told Jason Bitts I was going to ask Linda to marry me. I remember him looking at me like a deer in headlights and he barely said two words. I thought that was strange but it wasn't until later that I found out why.

"The game got off to a pretty good start. It was a real hard battle but we were up three to nothing. Saranac fumbled and we got the ball. Jason and I had this amazing play; he would fake to the right, run left and throw it to me as I ran down the sideline. It started like clockwork.

He made the fake, ran left to get clear just long enough to lob the ball my way. It was high, so I jumped up as high as I could and I caught it. It was one of those clean solid catches that I knew I was going to score.

"Then, I felt what seemed like a wall of bricks slam into me. My feet never hit the ground. Saranac had that moose of a guy, and he had been sticking pretty close to me the entire game. As I jumped for the ball, he took my legs out from under me. He tore the tendons in my right knee. I was out for the rest of the season. I was never able to play football any where near like I used to."

"I remember that game, Jonathan. You were robbed!"

"It sure felt like it," said John. "I sat there in that hospital bed, writhing in pain trying to make sense of what the doctor was telling me. I was able to gather myself together and figure that not all was lost because I still had Linda and still had that ring back in my locker to give her. Well, that night in the hospital Linda came to see me. I decided I was going to ask her to marry me right there in the hospital.

"Before I had a chance to ask her to marry me, she broke things off. She said she was sorry, but she loved someone else. She was in love with Jason, my best friend for God's sake!"

"Ouch, John. I never knew that."

"There is a point to my personal drama, Will," said John with a smirk. "Like you, Will, my life was torn apart in what seemed like a split second. I felt hopeless and like a failure. I saw nothing to look forward to and I felt like my life was spinning out of control. Everything I knew or trusted was not there anymore. I failed…I was not good enough…you name it—I believed it. Life was starting to look like a sick joke."

"Sick joke? What do you mean, John?" I asked.

"I guess I thought I was fooled into thinking I was smart and going places." Then Jonathan said something to me that I did not dare utter out loud myself, "Will, I thought God was betraying or punishing me somehow. I couldn't compete with someone that huge."

I was hoping to hear something that would give me faith again, faith in myself and in my Creator. "Yeah John, that is how I feel. How did you get passed it all?"

"Dad!" John stood up, walked over to the window and stared out of it as he continued. "After about a week, Dad pulled me aside, and he and I had a serious heart to heart talk."

Jonathan paused for a moment, cleared his throat and continued, "I remember Dad began our talk by saying, 'Life doesn't feel too good right now, does it Jonathan?' Dad sat there and waited for me to respond as if he had all the time in the world for me. I found myself needing to tell him.

"I told Dad that was exactly how I felt, that life was a joke and I did not see the point to it all. Dad looked me in the eye and gently said, 'Life doesn't always turn out the way we would like, and sometimes life seems down right cruel. There have been times in my life when I've felt just as you do. The most difficult moment of my life was losing Sarah. That's when life felt real cruel. My world came to a bitter halt. I just couldn't figure out why that had to happen to my beautiful little girl. Everything I believed in was called into question. I literally felt vulnerable to the evils of the world, as though I had no protection. Terrible things could happen to those I love, to me, and there wasn't a darn thing I could do about it. I could no longer recognize this God I had believed in all those years."

Will was surprised at his dad's honesty and how his feelings mirrored his own. "Jonathan, I know exactly what dad was feeling. That's me."

"Right," said Jonathan.

"How did Dad come to believe in God again?" I asked.

"Dad said he never stopped believing in God, instead he felt like he didn't know him anymore. Dad realized that his life with Sarah was a gift, no matter how long. How could he love Sarah so much, be thankful that he had her in his life and still deny her Creator? He knew he couldn't.

"Having faith in God means realizing He is good no matter what. Nothing can contradict that. It means believing He sympathizes with our weaknesses and forgives us even when we can't forgive ourselves. It also seems to mean that He will help us make sense of things, but until then, we are to try our best to trust Him. Life does not become meaningless because we can't figure it out anymore. Life is meaningful because God has a plan for each of us. Until then, we have to hold onto hope."

"Dad was pretty insightful," I said.

"Yeah. And thank God I didn't marry Linda, because then I wouldn't have met Susan, who just happens to be the perfect woman for me.

"If I had gone to Cal State, then who would have learned the business? Who would have been able to keep this mill running? The possibility is no one. All these men could have lost their job. Can you imagine three hundred men unemployed here in Kateyville? That would have been disastrous. Not only that, Will, I love it here at the mill! I was born to do this. This is a love both Dad and I share."

Jonathan smiled and then said, "You're growing up, Will. In fact, you kinda remind me of someone."

Curious, I asked, "Who? Who do I remind you of?"

"Dad," Jonathan answered.

"Thank you, Jonathan!" I figured saying anything more would ruin the moment, so I shook Jonathan's hand, gave a nod and turned to leave. I realized the gratitude that I felt for my brother, so I turned back and embraced Jonathan.

Chapter 32
Repentance

There were two stops I planned to make before going to see Lori. Facing her after all I put her through, took all the courage I could muster. Mom was right; it was important to me that we remain friends. We may never have a long-term relationship as I truly desired, but I can't imagine a life without Lori being in it in some capacity, without being her friend.

My first stop went much better than I thought it would. In fact, it was rather amazing and encouraging. It's as though God had decided to give me another chance, and the last thing I wanted to do was blow it.

Leaving my final destination, I felt energized and hopeful for the first time in a long time. The future may actually be brighter and more hopeful than I thought.

I ran back home and after grabbing Dad's hat from my bedroom, I jumped in his 1953 Buick Skylark convertible. I couldn't believe it, but Dad left his beautiful car to me, and I sure was honored. He gave it to me because he wanted me to enjoy it and drive it. Today, I finally decided I would do just that. After turning the ignition key, I let the Buick sit there for a while to get warmed up. She was my dad's pride and joy, and so, in the quiet of the car, I made a vow to my dad. "I know you loved this beauty. You showed that in the way you cared for her, washing and waxing her every chance you got. Well, Dad, I promise you today that I will take good care of her just as you did. You have my word." And with that, I put his hat on my head, put the car in gear, and slowly pulled out of the driveway.

Before I started down the street, I noticed Mom on the front porch. She had a very big smile on her face. I could tell she was proud and relieved that I had finally decided to drive Dad's car. She was probably thinking that it was the beginning of good things, that I had finally turned a corner in my life. Well, if that is what she was thinking, she was right.

Turning into Lori's driveway, I saw her sitting on the front porch reading a book. My sweet Lori did love to read! She picked her head up as I drove in, and I could tell she was shocked. Maybe she was even a bit happy; I thought, for sure, I could see her force back a smile.

Standing up, Lori began to speak, "Will, can I help you? Are you lost?"

Opening my car door, I stepped out, took my hat off and said, "No, Lori. I'm not lost. In fact, I think I'm right where I'm supposed to be; standing here, finally, facing you, and I must say, admiring you."

A confused scowl creased her brow. "Will, what's going on? Why did you come out here?"

Standing there, looking at Lori, I realized just how much I had missed her. From where I stood, I could smell the balsam shampoo she always used, along with the perfume I remembered, the one with the fragrances of jasmine and musk. While her scent brought me back to the past her present beauty did not go unnoticed. Her skin was the color of ivory with just a hint of tiny freckles sprinkled randomly across her nose. Today, she was wearing her hair down and her soft blond waves fell gently over her shoulders. I didn't remember it being so long, but I guess time causes many things to change. I just hoped her feelings hadn't.

While gazing at Lori, she interrupted, "Will, did you have something to say?"

This was going to be difficult, but I knew it was also too important to run away from. I began my apology, "Lori, I came to ask you to forgive me. I have been acting terrible, and I'm very sorry. Words can't make up for what I've done, shutting you out the way I have, but I hope it's a start. I also realize you may have moved on, dating other guys. If that's the case, I understand, but the last thing I want to lose is your friendship."

Now, Lori wore a face that was half between a scowl and a smile, bringing her hand to her mouth, and with bit of a chuckle she responded, "Moved on? Dating other guys? Will, what are you talking about?"

Oh boy, now I felt a little embarrassed. I didn't like showing my jealousy. "Well, you know what I mean, that guy you were with today…"

Lori's uproarious laughter stopped me mid sentence. Obviously delighting in my ignorance, she began to enlighten me. "That guy? That guy is my cousin, you goof! His name is Ronald Dune, and his father is my Uncle Gordon. When I saw you today, I knew that's what you thought. Thanks for all the confidence you have in me!" Lori said sarcastically. "Ronald and his parents have come here to stay with me for a couple of weeks because Dad had to go to Washington. He has a meeting at the Pentagon. With her laugh now fading, she said that her father would be gone for several weeks.

It was shocking to me that her father would leave Lori for such a long time. It seemed to be completely out of character for him, given how protective he was of her. "I bet he didn't like leaving you behind, did he?" I asked her.

"Actually, no, he didn't. You're right, Will. He was feeling a bit guilty about leaving me for so long, but he said if it wasn't for such an important reason, he would never have agreed to go. The only thing he could say was that the meeting in question was highly classified and rather sensitive in nature."

I was in awe and told her so, "Wow, that's impressive! You're dad is attending a meeting at the Pentagon!"

Lori thought my interest in her dad's exploits was great, but right now she wanted to get back to personal matters that were pending between us. "I don't fall out of love that easily, Will! I knew full well that once you learned about Sandy, you'd never be the same. I was worried how you would handle it, but I was determined to stand by you, no matter what. And I still feel that way. I also knew you still loved me, but the grief simply clouded your view. Believing in you comes naturally for me."

Stunned, I could hardly believe she loved me that much. She waited all that time, while I was being a complete jerk. "Lori, you amaze me. I can't believe you're still willing to stand by me after all I've put you through. I've never felt this way about any other girl. I never stopped loving you." As I was talking, my feet found their way to her, and soon we were facing each other.

Lori looked up at me with those amazing sapphire eyes and responded to all I had said, "William Casey, I love you with all my heart."

Ever so carefully, my arms embraced Lori. I felt as if I could have stood there like that for ever. There was no other place I wanted to be.

Soon, Lori asked me to come into the house and meet her aunt and uncle and her cousin, Ronald. I found them to be warm and hospitable. I was confident they would take good care of Lori while her dad was away. It was also evident that their rules mirrored those of Lori's dad. Before I left, I asked Lori and Ronald if they would like to come for dinner on Friday night.

After they accepted the invitation, Lori walked me to the car. I slid behind the steering wheel of my car, and was about to drive away, when Lori said she had a question for me. "What made you finally decide to drive your dad's car?" she asked.

"I have finally decided to live, Lori! Things happen that hurt, things we can't change, but we can't stop living, and we can't stop believing that good things are yet to come. The circumstances of life can shape us in many ways, good or bad. I've decided to look for the good."

With a look that let me know how pleased she was, Lori added, "Well, I do declare, Mr. William Casey, you most certainly have grown up these last few months. I'm very impressed! By the way, that car looks mighty impressive on you, as well."

And with that, I placed Dad's hat on my head, gave Lori a wink, and drove off.

Chapter 33
Sandy's Ashes

As I drove home from Lori's, I mused over the many important events of the day. My mission of repentance was finally put into action and into words. To my great relief, Jonathan and Lori accepted my apologies. After seeing Jonathan, I also went to see Gregg, knowing that I owed him a proper explanation for my distant behavior as well. He, like the others, kindly forgave me.

The purpose for talking with Gregg was two fold. Not only did I go with the intention of apologizing for my recent, repulsive behavior, but also to inquire about the whereabouts of two special horses, the foals Sandy sired. Whatever it took, I wanted to bring them home. Thankfully, Gregg knew where they were. Before I knew it, I was heading out of town toward the next county to meet with the family who had been raising them.

Later that evening, I pulled into the driveway and carefully parked Dad's car in the garage and headed inside. Mom was in the kitchen preparing dinner, and boy did it smell good! In the air was the savory aroma of pork loin baking in Mom's famous honey-maple, mustard sauce. Mashed potatoes were kept warm on the stove along side a pot of homegrown string beans and corn. A batch of her renowned, chocolate chip, pecan cookies were appetizingly displayed on the counter. My mouth began to salivate at the anticipation of such a great meal.

"Hello, Mom, how was your day?" I asked.

"Refreshingly ordinary; how was yours? I have a feeling it was far from ordinary. Am I right?" she inquisitively asked.

Mom had been extremely curious ever since she saw me come out of the barn this morning with that eureka- type look on my face. Her self-control was amazing. She acted calm and collected, as though I could answer her if I chose to, but it wasn't all that necessary. She pretended she really wasn't all that interested, so I decided to dangle my answer a bit before divulging all the details. "Oh, not too much happened today. I saw Jonathan, Gregg and Lori, but that's about it. Oh yeah, I did visit a family in the next county, but other than that, my day was pretty ordinary, just like yours, I guess. I'm going to go wash up for dinner, and I'll grab the boys and have them do the same. See you at dinner."

That little stinker, Mom said to herself. *I'll bet he knows full well I'm beside myself with curiosity! I'll just have to wait it out. For goodness' sake, I've waited this long to see him happy; the reason can wait.*

Christopher and Lenny were playing with their Matchbox cars upstairs, so I rounded them up and told them to get ready for dinner. Before long, all of us, except Shannon, were in the kitchen doing our best to help Mom get dinner on the table. "Where is Shannon, Mom?" I asked.

"She's gone out for pizza and a movie with her girlfriends. She won't be back until ten or so," Mom answered.

Now that I wasn't so self-absorbed, I was really curious about her and Bart. I suspected Bart always liked my sister, but I had no idea Shannon felt the same. I wonder how all that came about? One thing's for sure; it happened when I was in the hospital, probably while I was sleeping my life away. I suppose if they're happy, then I'll be happy too. But it does seem weird. Maybe I'll ask Mom about them, and see what she thinks about the whole thing. "Um, Mom, what's going on between Shannon and Bart? Are they dating, or are they just friends?"

Mom never liked to discuss the private affairs of one child with another, unless, of course, it proved necessary. I knew I wouldn't get much out of her, but I decided to ask anyway. "Bart and your sister?

You'll have to ask Shannon about that. I will tell you one thing; they get along famously."

Some help that was, but it was about what I expected.

Mom was eager to get dinner started, "Okay, everyone, have a seat at the table. Mom asked Lenny if he would like to say grace tonight, and he was excited to do so. "Lord, bless this food. Amen."

Short and sweet, just the way I liked it when my stomach was growling. I know, I know, pretty selfish, but a guy doesn't change completely over night, right?

Finally, I decided to tell Mom about my day. When I had finished telling her everything, her hand stretched across the table to grab mine, and she gave it a squeeze. "You're a special boy, William. You have good things ahead; I can feel it. Now eat."

Dinner tomorrow night was going to be special, and after I told Mom all the people I invited, she thought it would be special too. In fact, she said she was looking forward to it. Plans were already being made for tomorrow evening's menu. While eating our dinner, we decided what we should serve. It was unanimous; Mom would prepare London broil, salt potatoes, vegetable salad and corn-on-the-cob. We couldn't agree on what we should have for dessert, so one of us had to compromise. I figured it should be me since Mom was the one cooking everything. I wanted banana-cream pie, but Mom didn't feel it was as popular as apple pie. So, apple pie it was.

After dinner, I helped Mom clear the table and offered to do the dishes. While I washed, she dried, and we took this special time to talk about Sandy. "The day of my race was traumatic, wasn't it Mom?"

"Yes, Will, it sure was. In only a few short minutes, I thought my son would die, and I knew Sandy would. Saying goodbye to Sandy was very hard, but at the time I was so worried about you that I didn't allow myself to absorb it completely, not until, that is, Mr. Pace came by the hospital. He was really shaken up, but the biggest thing he was concerned about was you and how you would handle Sandy being gone, never being able to truly say goodbye. Gregg remarked that even that was taken from you. He felt helpless, understanding that so many things were out of our control that day. It was a day of horrible circumstances, to say the least.

Making plans to properly say goodbye to Sandy was on my mind. "Mom, where are Sandy's ashes? I'd like to have them."

With a knowing and sympathetic look, she told me where I could find Sandy's ashes. I excused myself and set out to get them. I began to make special plans, proper plans, to say goodbye to an old friend. I would begin to carry out those plans very early, before sunrise.

Chapter 34
Saying Goodbye to an Old Friend

Before going to bed, I decided to do something that was long overdue and something I was sure my father did. He was never ashamed of this ritual, and that left a huge impression on me. I slowly fell to my knees and said a prayer. I asked God to bless my family and friends and to forgive me for shutting so many out of my life, including Him.

I thought of the many times Mom tucked us kids into bed and said our prayers with us. She told us there was no better way to end the day. I think she was right.

Once I finished fumbling over the words of my prayer, I got into bed. From where I lay, I could see the box on the dresser filled with Sandy's ashes. The box was made of cedar wood and was ornamented with a gold plate inscribed with Sandy's name. Next to the small box containing his ashes was my alarm clock, set to go off at five a.m. Exhausted, I put my head down on my pillow, and within moments, I was sound asleep.

Opening my eyes, I could hardly believe it was morning already. I think the events of yesterday really knocked me out; I slept like a baby. My sheets and blankets were not disheveled and tangled as they usually were. This was very uncommon for me; usually by morning most of my bedding was on the floor.

Looking over at the cedar box filled with Sandy's ashes, I noticed the alarm hadn't yet gone off. So, before it had a chance to wake anyone, I got up and turned the timer off. I rubbed my hand across my face as I thought of Sandy. Picking up the cedar box, I brushed my thumb across the engraved gold plate. Feelings of grief and loneliness began to come over me; my heart ached at the realization he was really gone. For so many years, Sandy was a part of my life, and I guess in some ways, he will always be.

I set the box down and got dressed. Once I found my dad's hat and a jacket, I grabbed the gold plated box, and headed down to the kitchen.

The ritual began. First, I grabbed three doughnuts, a mug of milk and three sugar cubes. It was still dark when I stepped outside and headed for the barn. I began to talk to Sandy. "Well, boy. This is it. I'm sorry it has taken me so long to properly say goodbye; I guess I didn't have the strength until now." Quietly, I finished the walk to the barn. Going inside, I walked into Sandy's stall and took in the fresh scent of hay. I dragged my hand along the stall door, and then found my way to his saddle hanging from a nail near the top of the roughly hewed walls. Touching that saddle, smelling the leather, and closing my eyes allowed me to imagine that Sandy was right there beside me. I stood there for quite some time recollecting his scent, his face and his gentle presence. Like viewing a movie, vivid images flashed across my mind. I remembered times when Sandy and I raced with the wind, across meadows and along the Raquette River. I feared there would never be a time such as that again.

I opened my eyes and said, "Well, Sandy, let's go take in the sunrise together, one more time." I carried Sandy's ashes to a nearby hill.

The wind was blowing so hard, that Dad's hat nearly blew off my head. I could feel a light sprinkle in the air, and the cold air seemed to find its way to my very bones. I shivered in the morning mist.

Finding our favorite spot, I sat on the ground waiting for the sun to rise. After placing the cedar box next to me, I grabbed the three sugar cubes from my pocket and placed them on top. I reached for the doughnuts in my other pocket and proceeded to dunk them in my milk. Our world was quiet, except for the soft rustle of the wind and the tiny drip, drip of rain falling on my jacket and the cedar box.

In the stillness, I felt Sandy standing right next to me; so much so, that I strained my eyes to see him through the darkness. But there was only the reality of loss and darkness about me.

After finishing my final doughnut, I could see the sun begin to climb above the horizon. This was my cue. Taking the cedar box in my hand, I stood up and opened it. As I did, overwhelming grief filled my soul. I knew this was our final goodbye, and the finality of it seemed unbearable. "Well, Sandy, here we are enjoying another sunrise together, just like we have so many times in the past. This is my first sunup since the accident, and your last, a defining moment for us both; wouldn't you say? You have been my loyal friend, and I will never forget you." For a long moment, I stood quiet.

"Sandy, I have a favor to ask of you. When you meet Sarah up there in Heaven, would you have Dad place her on your back? Take her for a ride around Heaven. Be her friend and companion, just as you have been mine. I wish there was a way for you to let her know how much I love her and how sorry I am for being so mean to her that day, the day at the beach. If I could change anything in my life, that would be it."

I paused for what seemed a long time, watching the sun move its way up in the sky. I then spoke my final goodbye.

Upon opening the box, I noticed that the wind had picked up speed. As I began to dump Sandy's ashes over the field below, the wind suddenly grew fierce. A large gust of air grabbed Sandy's ashes and spread them as far as the eye could see. And with tears in my eyes, I shouted, "God speed, dear Sandy, God speed!" And as he often did in life, Sandy ran free with the wind, across the field.

I didn't leave until every last ash was out of sight. And once the wind took everything away, the drizzle of the rain turned to a downpour. I looked up at the heavens, closed my eyes, and as the rain washed over me, I imagined Sarah riding on Sandy's back with my Dad cheering them on. I welcomed the soaking rain and allowed it to drench me through and through, body and soul. The rain brought with it a sense of peace and a type of knowing. For the first time in a long time, I believed I was going to be okay. I knew I was beginning to believe there was Someone in control, even if I wasn't. There has to be a Creator; how else could there have been an animal as magnificent as Sandy? A soul as beautiful as his has to live on, somewhere.

Chapter 35
Charlie and Sugar

When I got back to the house, Mom was sitting at the table drinking her coffee and reading her paper.

"Good morning, Mom," I said.

"Good morning, Will. I had a feeling you would be out before this morning's sunrise. Did you say goodbye to Sandy? When I saw you leave with his ashes this morning, I had a pretty good idea what you were going to do." Mom's inquiry was gentle and reassuring.

"It was difficult and very sad, almost like my heart got broken all over again, but it was also a beautiful reminder of what we had. Having Sandy in my life was a tremendous blessing. He taught me more about life than most adults could. Surprisingly, Mom, I feel a sense of peace after saying goodbye.

It was time I got ready for my day ahead. I had a few things I needed to take care of before tonight's dinner. After taking a very hot shower and eating my breakfast, I headed for the kitchen door. Before I left, I asked Mom if I could pick up anything at the store for her. She told me that she had the dinner preparations under control, and with that, I told her I would see her later.

Before heading for Saranac, I picked up the horse trailer from Gregg's house and prepared it for the now, full-grown, quarter horses. I saw them only briefly yesterday, and I couldn't get over how much they reminded me of Sandy, especially Charlie. Sandy had those bright, perceptive eyes that revealed his keen understanding of people and events around him. Charlie had those same intelligent, sharp eyes.

The Stellars had an amazing ranch nestled in the Adirondack Mountains. It was located very close to Saranac Lake, a picturesque, mountainous, North-Country community. A white, painted fence stretched out as far as the eye could see, across a grand landscape. In fact, it was a place so beautiful, with its mammoth size barn, rolling hills, and magnificent scenery that I almost felt guilty about taking Charlie and Sugar away from it all.

As I drove down the Stellar's driveway toward their impressive ranch, I could see them waving to me from their front porch. They had been expecting me by eight o'clock, and I was just a couple of minutes early. Mark Stellar waved me on to the barn where Charlie and Sugar were. Before I knew it, Mark and Holly Stellar's five children came running out, wanting to know what was going on. They had lots of questions for me, and from the sounds of it, they seemed to already know who I was.

The oldest boy, Hadean, began, "Hey, are you that Will guy that got in the horse accident in Kateyville? We were there you know; my two brothers and I…well, we thought you were dead."

Surprised by his honesty, I answered him, "Yes, that was me."

"I'm sure glad you didn't die, Mr.!" said Steven, the middle boy.

"Me too!" I said with a chuckle. We all got a big laugh out of Steven's candidness.

Before long, Mark and I had the horses boarded, and we were ready to go. Shaking his hand, I thanked him for all he had done and asked if they would like to visit us at our ranch in Kateyville. Mark told me they would be sure to stop by when they were in the area. Driving away, something inside me told me we'd see each other again. They were kind people, and I felt as if I had known them for a long time.

While driving down the Stellar's long driveway, I turned around and glanced at the horses riding behind me. There was a wonderful realization that Sandy would live on through these horses, just as a part of my dad lives on in me. Seeing these two creatures, I was able to peer through the window of my future, a future that looked brighter with each passing day. I could hardly wait until the others got the chance to see them. I yelled to my fellow travelers, "Sugar! Charlie! Let's go home!"

Once home, I spent the entire day getting to know my new friends. Both were the color of chestnut, had good lines, and supported themselves with a strong muscular build. It wasn't until I got on the back of Charlie, that I realized what an amazing runner he was. He had Sandy's stride, his amazing start time and that incredible racing stamina. He raced with such passion and perseverance; it was like riding Sandy. The adrenaline rush I felt was glorious. "Yeee Haw!" was all my mouth could say as we barreled across the field.

Checking my watch, I realized my friends would be arriving soon, and I needed to go and make some preparations. Leaving those thoroughbred beauties wasn't easy, but I needed to get back to the house. Walking back, I spoke softly to Sandy, because if he truly was in heaven, as I believed, I knew he could here me. "Your children are gorgeous and amazing just like you. Sugar is a good name for Charlie's little sister; she has a real sweet temperament. She's not the fastest runner, but she has a beautiful stride. That Charlie on the other hand, he's a real runner. He's got your stride and your speed, Sandy, and did you see his starting time? He reminds me of you! What do you think? They're fine horses, and they would make you proud."

With that, I headed towards the house.

Chapter 36
Abiding Hope

After looking at my hands and clothes, I decided to take a quick shower before our guests arrived. While passing Mom in the kitchen, I could tell exactly what she was thinking. "Don't worry, Mom, I'm heading straight for the shower. When I'm finished, I'll come down and help you."

While leaving the room, with what sounded like a bit of a giggle, I heard her say under her breath, "Thank goodness! He smells like Mr. Bailey's dairy farm."

The first to arrive was Jonathan and Susan. Susan wanted to come a bit early and help if it was needed. Although, now that Susan was pregnant, she'd be lucky if my mom let her bring something as heavy as a fork to the table. Mom said that when a woman is pregnant, she should be able to take it easy, but when the woman is Susan and she's pregnant with her grandchild, she deserves excessive pampering. Susan didn't see it that way; she felt fine and wanted to help. So, Mom said she would give in this time and let Jonathan and Susan set the table.

Soon, everybody was coming through the door, Bart, Gregg and then Lori with her cousin, Ronald. For about an hour, we all stood around the kitchen talking, enjoying each other's company, but soon it was time to eat. In front of each place setting, Mom had written a person's name on a little card. She told each of us to find our name and take a seat. Mom always knew how to put the finishing touches on things.

Once we were all seated, Mom asked if I would say grace. We held hands and bowed our heads. "Dear Lord, thank You for this beautiful dinner my mom has so generously made. Bless her, Lord, for her kindness. I also ask You, Heavenly Father, to please bless each of my friends here tonight. They have been loyal and true friends. Thank You for our many blessings, dear Lord," and making the sign of the cross, "It's in the name of the Father, Son and Holy Spirit, Amen."

Looking around the table, I remarked to myself how fortunate I was to have such amazing friends. Bart has been my loyal friend since kindergarten, and I am incredibly proud to call him friend. Putting up with my bad temper and my rather rebellious actions all these years wasn't easy, but still, he remained my loyal friend. He has an air of self-confidence and a fun-loving nature that makes him enjoyable to be around. Very often, Bart works hard at covering up his softer, caring side. He's like a brother to me; he's a great guy. And if he's truly fond of my sister, I couldn't be happier.

Shannon has become a remarkable young lady, confident to the core. Many would say, "Who wouldn't be if they looked like that?" Well, I don't think her confidence comes from that (her looks that is) but rather from the inside. I have seen many people who, even though they are attractive, lack confidence, and I have seen some who weren't especially good-looking, who still carried themselves with obvious self-assurance.

My mom and my dad often told Shannon that she could achieve anything in her life she was willing to work for. Growing up with four brothers, my mom didn't want her lost in a sea of male dominance. She never wanted her to lose the true sense of who she was, and I believe that whatever my mom did, she certainly helped Shannon accomplish that.

Now, Gregg is a unique and interesting man, always extremely reserved and not much for conversation, but when things had to be said, he said them. He is a man of incredible insight when it comes to horses and racing, but he is not a man prone to boasting about his vast horse sense.

Given the way he often dressed around the track, many visitors often mistook him for one of the stable hands, responsible for cleaning up after the horses. Whenever one of those pompous types talked down to him, I had all I could do not to lose my temper and let them know just who it was they were talking to—a well respected horse trainer. Around here, he was known as one of the best. But would Gregg tell them that? Never! He was always polite and said very little. More often than not, Gregg helped those people with whatever it was they bothered him about in the first place. I'll never forget the incident last year when one of those well-to-do's treated Gregg like the manure found in the tread of my shoes. The man wanted him to bend over and pick up some trash the man's wife had dropped. Looking at Gregg, I so desperately wanted him to give the guy a piece of his mind, but he didn't. After picking up the rubbish, Gregg actually asked the guy if he would like him to throw it away for him. In a tone that made my hair curl, the guy said, "Do with it what you want. That's your job, isn't it?" Just as all this was happening, a track employee spotted Gregg and called his name loud enough for this overweight, rude man and his wife to hear. "Gregg Pace, Mr. Pace, Sir! Could you help us with one of the horses, Sir? We realize it's not one of yours, but we could really use your expertise on this one. Would you mind, Mr. Pace?"

Well, anyone who knows anything about horses around here knows the name Gregg Pace, and that included the rude man and his wife. That man turned shades of pink and then red; he was completely embarrassed. While trying to apologize, Gregg just tipped his hat to the man and walked away, never saying a word.

After Gregg left, the guy looked at me as if to say sorry, but I just shook my head and walked away. Impertinence sure is ugly.

There's this proverb I remember from church school that sums up Gregg Pace, and I think it goes like this, "A wise man holds his tongue. Only a fool blurts out everything he knows; that only leads to trouble." So, when I think of Gregg, I think of a wise man with vast knowledge and a patient, kind heart. He is a loyal friend; I don't know what I would do without him.

Looking across the table at Jonathan, I remembered back to yesterday, when his love for me was gently and compassionately displayed. After telling him about Sarah, he didn't blame or condemn. I'm fortunate to have a brother like him, someone to look up to and confide in, especially now that Dad isn't here for such things. I now know that no matter what transpires, he will be there for me and our entire family. He's done a great job, stepping in where Dad left off. Of course, he probably would not see it that way. I know Jonathan well, and I'll bet, in his mind, he just doesn't feel worthy of being compared to Dad. If that's the case, he's wrong. He's going to be a wonderful father to this new baby of his, just like Dad was. I sure hope this legacy of extraordinary father will, somehow, be passed on to all of us guys.

The boys, Christopher and Lenny, let's face it, they would bring joy to anyone's life. Christopher loves playing with dump trucks and tractors and said that one day he wants to be a tractor-trailer driver. Big for his age, he is the brother who often protects little Lenny. As it turns out, Christopher is known as the tough and rough Casey kid, and Lenny is known for being the Casey who is nice to everyone. Christopher doesn't seem to mind what people think of him, as long as no one picks on Lenny.

Lenny is small, but, boy, what a power house, a firecracker with an amazing sense of humor; that's Lenny. If Lenny is in a room, people are laughing. It could be one of his witty sayings, his crazy, rubber-band-like dancing or a hilarious body pose. He sure knows how to light up a room.

Every child has their favorite toys, and for Lenny it's his boats. He loves sail boats and big navel ships best, and swears that one day he will be in the navy. Somehow, I believe he will; he just happens to have that certainty about him. He often answers questions with a unique phrase all his own, "You betcha!"

Lori looks so pretty tonight. She's kind, witty and smart. I've never felt this way about any other girl; I truly hope there is a future for us. Even though we will be going in different directions this fall, I never want to lose her.

Lori's intelligence impresses me, and I believe she can accomplish anything she sets her mind to. She will make a fine doctor someday, if that's her desire. It's important to me that she go after her dreams.

Tonight, after I introduce everyone to Charlie and Sugar, I hope to tell Lori about my plans.

There hasn't been a woman, until Lori, who could hold my attention. It's not that there weren't a lot of nice girls around; I simply wasn't interested. Racing and rodeo were my main passions, and they consumed much of my time and thinking. Then along came Lori, and for some reason, she grabbed my attention right away and sparked my interest. After meeting her, I knew I had to get to know her better. I couldn't have been happier the day I discovered she cared for me as well. Much like me, however, she didn't want anyone interfering with her plans. I understood that all too well, but fate seemed to rule in my favor the day Lori professed her love for me. One can't know the future, but one can hope, and I hope for a future that includes her.

Sitting at the other end of the table, is my Mom. What a remarkable woman! Don't let that kind, caring, disposition fool you; she could run General Motors single handedly. Seeing her remain strong and stable through the frustrations of life has impressed me greatly. I marvel at her self-control. When she is upset, angry or sad, she never allows her feelings to become an excuse for mistreating someone. She understands the power of words and knows they often have far-reaching influence and consequences. A hasty, uncontrolled remark can cause a child to feel unloved, a friend to feel rejected, a spouse to feel under-appreciated or a stranger to think unkindly of her. No matter how many times we may have gotten ourselves into trouble, and Mom had to punish us, we still always knew she loved us.

Standing up from my chair, I clanged my glass with a fork. The table went silent. "Hello, guys! Thanks for coming tonight. This evening has some special meaning for me, and I wanted to share it with all of you. First, thank you for accepting my apologies. I have been quite the jerk lately, but I'm proud to say that my life has taken a turn for the better. Something happened to me recently that made me realize just how much I had given up by shutting each of you out of my life." I passed a small glance toward Lori, and gave her a tiny wink.

"I have begun to think about what is important. All of you are at the top of my list, but another thing has also been on my mind. I wanted to find the two horses that Sandy sired. It was something Dad wanted to do before he left us. Mom told me about the foals, but I didn't give it that much thought because I had Sandy, and we were preparing for the big race. While preparing for the race, as all of you may remember, my mind didn't seem to want to focus on anything else.

"And then came the accident, and I…we lost Sandy. That's when I decided I wanted them; I wanted to be able to hold on to Sandy somehow."

I was starting to get a bit choked up, so I paused for a minute, and then continued, "As you guys know, I finally became aware of my self-serving attitude, and I knew things had to change. I have never been the type of person who liked to hurt people, and I knew this was no time to start. Just because I was hurting, that didn't give me an excuse to hurt others. I thought about my dad, and I realized he would never have acted the way I did. Dad set a much better example than I was following. What he began, in spite of his father, was something to be proud of. Our dad 'took back the land', so to speak. He wasn't going to let his father's mistakes set a precedent for him. Dad wanted more for us and himself than that. To do that, it took a willing heart and a wise and very unselfish man."

I looked at Jonathan as I continued, "I could see that Jonathan was living a life that honored Dad and his accomplishments, and I want to do the same."

I turned my gaze to the others at the table as I spoke, "When I began thinking about Dad's gift to us, I was reminded of Sandy's. Don't forget, Sandy is the bloodline of Jackson, Dad's beloved horse. It was then I knew I must find Sandy's foals, and I'm proud to say they're here, in our barn. I'm sure it's no surprise to you, however, that they are no longer foals. I invited all of you here tonight so I could introduce you to them. So, guys, please follow me, and let me introduce you to some fine thoroughbred's."

Mom told everyone to go out to the barn, and she would join them later. There were many objections; no one wanted to leave her with all of those dirty dishes. But, Mom wouldn't have it any other way. She said it was her kitchen, and according to her, she decides what goes on there.

Walking out, I grabbed Lori's hand. Out of the corner of my eye, I saw Bart grab Shannon's. "There you have it," I said to Lori. "They're an item. Well, good for them; I think they make a great pair, don't you?"

Lori smiled in their direction, and said, "Most definitely!"

Opening the barn door, we were greeted by two very content-looking horses. I eagerly introduced them. "This is Sugar; she's the female and extremely sweet tempered, and this is Charlie, a runner like his dad."

"Will, this is great! Are you going to race them?" Shannon asked.

"I've made some plans for myself, as well as these two beautiful, quarter horses. It looks like I'm going back to school. I know, I know; you can't believe I would choose to go back to school, but it's true. But that's not all! I've talked to the guys at the track, and they're going to let me start a racing and rodeo school for young boys who want to ride competitively. This year is looking great, and I'm really looking forward to it."

Lori looked at Will, and with obvious excitement said, "Will, I'm really proud of you; you'll be the best teacher ever! But I have to say that I'm also a bit curious. I thought you didn't really like school. What made you change your mind? And what are you going to go to school for?"

Would they really believe me? I was sure they would be stunned when I announced that I wanted to be a veterinarian. Needless to say, they were surprised, knowing my previous lack of interest in school, but they were also very supportive. My plans were to go to a two-year college nearby, and then later transfer to Cornell University.

"What made you decide that's what you wanted to do?" asked Bart.

It was now time to reveal the life-lesson I had learned, the one my mom knew I needed to discover on my own, "Well, Bart it was a combination of things, really. I realized it was easy to be strong when everything around me was going well, but I lacked the inner strength to keep steady when times got tough. I needed something more, something to believe in.

"As you all know, the Caseys are people who try to live good lives, you know, live by Christian principles. For so many years, I went through the motions, but I never allowed myself to believe, much less begin to commit to what I had been taught. And then one day I realized something. The people I cared for the most lived by those principles in their everyday lives. People like Mom, Jonathan, and Shannon. Even the boys, Christopher and Lenny, lived a life that inspired me. Their actions spoke volumes about their strong, inner beliefs. But the one person I thought of most was my dad. He grew up with no parents, but thanks to his grandparents, he did experience a love and a faith that helped mold his life.

"I'll tell you something, if my family had not demonstrated such persistent and extraordinary love for me, I would not have bought this whole faith in God thing. I don't want anyone to think I'm trying to be all 'preachy'; I just want to get across to you what caused this hard heart of mine to change. Now, understand, I'm no Father Ray Mendez or anything, and I'm not going to go become a priest."

Looking at Lori, everyone saw her wipe her brow as if to say, "Whew." Everyone got a chuckle out of that.

I took a deep breath and continued, "So many things seemed to go wrong in my life, Sarah and Dad's death, and then Sandy. I got real angry and confused. For the life of me, I couldn't figure out how or why these things happened? I felt like God either didn't exist, or if he did, he didn't care. But then, somehow, I began to realize that since the beginning of time, bad things have always happened. Who was I to think that I should be exempted from trouble? Was I going to allow the circumstances of my life to cause me to give up? My Dad sure didn't. He remained faithful and refused to give up hope. Because of the beliefs burning within him, he wanted to pass that same heritage on to us. All we have to do is accept it. It's up to us to pass this hope on to future generations yet to come. And when you look around, you can see he was rewarded for his faithfulness. We have a family to be proud of, a future to look forward to, and a legacy to pass on to our children.

Through Dad's example, I have seen the results of a man living his life daring to hope, and in so doing, he found a faith that has molded a generation. I want to be like that man, my dad, who was willing to believe in something beyond himself. Human nature and pride are often sufficient for a crisis, but it takes grace to be exceptional in ordinary things. I want to live a life of courage, daring to hope in good things ahead.

Things Yet to Come

Now understand; things don't end here. So much has yet to happen. Does Will finally get that degree, and will Lori become a doctor? What will become of their romance? Can what they have last beyond their teenage years? What about the Rodeo School, does it become a huge success? Do the Casey's suffer more tragedy? Can Will pass on his new found faith and hope to future generations and to other hurting souls? Who is that little girl Will finds hiding in the stables?

What will become of Sugar and Charlie? Does Will make sure to keep their legacy alive and have more foals sired? I'll tell you one thing, Charlie sure makes the news!

What will happen to Bart and Shannon? Does their relationship flourish or fail? And how does Will handle his best friend being sent off to war? Does Bart return, and if he does, does he return the same?

I can tell that you are very curious about what the future holds for Will, his family, and friends. I will divulge a scant amount of information about a few future events. Cayey Lane does undergo some changes; a new doctor's office comes to town and so does a new, 'hoppin-good-time' restaurant with live music. I believe the name of this place is called Claire's. And get a hold of those new pencil skirts! The female mold is about to be broken.

Does Susan have a boy or a girl, or does she have both? What must Jonathan and Susan overcome if their marriage is to succeed? What happened to Susan that she and Jonathan must overcome?

A terrible accident at the mill brings the entire town to a standstill. What causes the fatal event, and was it done on purpose or was it just the "perfect storm?"

Will we ever know?
Maybe.

Bonnie's Dad, William Ford, at age 11

William Ford on right, Butch Murray on left.
In the novel, Bart Murray protrays Butch.

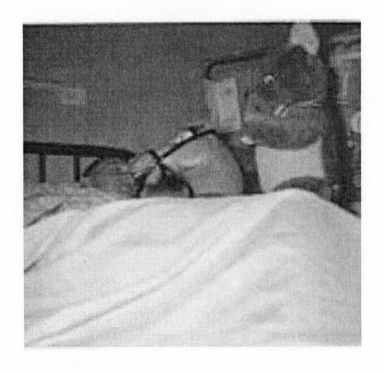

Bonnie's dad, William Ford, (or 'Billy' as many liked to call him) in his hospital bed after waking from his 17 day coma.

Bonnie's parents, William and Lorraine Ford, at the fair.
(Lorraine's maiden name is Dunning.)

Harry Ford, William Ford's dad, second one in from the right.
A ground breaking ceremony in their small town of Colton.